The Bartolini Legacy

A secret, an inheritance, a journey to happy-ever-after!

A diary...

After their parents' sudden deaths, the Bartolini siblings Bianca, Gia and Enzo return home to Tuscany and discover one of them is illegitimate!

A will...

As they're reeling from the bombshell, the will is read. The luxury family estate will be left to the sibling who can generate the greatest income.

A summer to remember...

While they wait for the DNA test results, each sibling embarks on their own vision for the vineyard's future. They have six months that will take them on a journey of self-discovery and finding love along the way...

Read Bianca's story in *The Prince and the Wedding Planner.*

And look out for Gia's and Enzo's stories Coming soon!

Dear Reader,

Sometimes it's a choice to change your life—such as starting your own wedding business. Other times, change can be thrust upon you with a phone call or, in this case, the turn of a page.

Wedding planner Bianca Bartolini's life has been thrown into a series of cascading changes when she returns to Tuscany for her parents' funeral. Yet when she uncovers her mother's journal, she comes across a bombshell of a secret. The words on those weathered pages put everything she and her brother and sister know about themselves, their parents and their relationships into question.

Crown Prince Leopold's younger sister is getting married, but what should be a joyous occasion is anything but harmonious. Leo needs some peace and quiet if he is ever to choose a wife—a mandated requirement before he can be crowned king. And then he latches on to the idea of hiring wedding planner Bianca—someone who will report to him and bring peace back to the palace...

Being a wedding planner to the royal family is a dream come true for Bianca. But will her family's secrets ruin her chance at happiness? And with Bianca's help, will Leo find the perfect princess?

Happy reading,

Jennifer

The Prince and the Wedding Planner

Jennifer Faye

ISBN-13: 978-1-335-55618-9

The Prince and the Wedding Planner

This edition published by arrangement with Harlequin Books S.A.

For questions and comments about the quality of this book, please contact us at CustomerService@Harlequin.com.

Harlequin Enterprises ULC
22 Adelaide St. West, 40th Floor
Toronto, Ontario M5H 4E3, Canada
www.Harlequin.com

Printed in U.S.A.

Award-winning author **Jennifer Faye** pens fun, heartwarming contemporary romances with rugged cowboys, sexy billionaires and enchanting royalty. Internationally published, with books translated into nine languages, she is a two-time winner of the *RT Book Reviews* Reviewers' Choice Award. She has also won the CataRomance Reviewers' Choice Award, been named a Top Pick author and been nominated for numerous other awards.

Books by Jennifer Faye

Harlequin Romance

Greek Island Brides

Carrying the Greek Tycoon's Baby
Claiming the Drakos Heir
Wearing the Greek Millionaire's Ring

The Cattaneos' Christmas Miracles

Heiress's Royal Baby Bombshell

Once Upon a Fairytale

Beauty and Her Boss
Miss White and the Seventh Heir

Mirraccino Marriages

The Millionaire's Royal Rescue
Married for His Secret Heir

Her Festive Baby Bombshell
Snowbound with an Heiress
Her Christmas Pregnancy Surprise

Visit the Author Profile page
at Harlequin.com for more titles.

Praise for Jennifer Faye

"Ms. Jennifer Faye always delivers the most poignant romantic stories. Romance is in the air and the ending is truly heartwarming for everyone. *Claiming the Drakos Heir* is Ms. Faye's best book, yet!"

—*Goodreads*

PROLOGUE

February, Tuscany, Italy

THIS WAS A living nightmare.

Bianca creaked open the door to her parents' bedroom. She peered inside, just like she used to do when she was a little girl. She paused as though waiting to be bid entrance. That would never happen.

Bianca tentatively stepped into the room, her gaze hungrily taking in her surroundings. The bed was made just as her mother left it each morning. There was still an indentation on her father's pillow as though his head had just been there—as though he would return to it that evening.

But that wasn't to be the case.

Her parents had died. The acknowledgment made her heart clench. One minute they'd been vibrant and active. In the next moment, they'd died in a horrific vehicle accident.

They hadn't been going anywhere special. It hadn't been a special day. It had been a perfectly ordinary day on a perfectly ordinary ride to the city to do some ordinary shopping. And yet it had ended with extraordinarily horrific results.

The backs of Bianca's eyes burned with unshed tears. She blinked repeatedly and sniffled. She had to pull herself together. Falling apart now wouldn't help anyone.

The funeral had just concluded and the will was to be read shortly. Everything was being pushed into fast forward as the vineyard had to be maintained. Springtime would soon be here and work would kick into high gear. Without someone in charge, the Barto Vineyard would suffer—her father's legacy would languish. His precious prize-winning grapes would wither on the vine.

The family's attorney thought with the vineyard at stake, it was reason enough to push her and her two siblings to read the will today of all days—while she was still wearing her black dress from the funeral, while the estate was still filled with mourners that had come to pay their respects.

All Bianca wanted to do that day was remember her parents—to bask in the love that lived within the walls of this vast villa. She pushed the door closed before stepping further into the bedroom. It was here, within her parents' suite of rooms, she felt closest to them.

It was here that her mother showed her how to put on makeup for the first time. It was here that her father had told her she could go away to university in the UK. Bianca walked around the spacious room, running her fingers over her mother's elaborately carved dresser with the huge mirror suspended above it.

She picked up her mother's silver hairbrush and noticed the few long dark strands of hair tangled around the bristles. The last of her mother. Tears clouded Bianca's vision as she thought of never seeing her parents ever again. It still seemed so utterly inconceivable.

She kept walking around the room, her fingers tracing over all the things, that until just days ago, her parents had touched—had used. The thought tugged on her heart strings. How could they be here one moment and then gone the next?

Bianca pressed a shaky hand to her mouth, holding back a wave of emotion that threatened to drown her in unbearable sorrow. She struggled to make sense of it. Why had they been stolen away when they were still so vital—still so needed? When she still didn't have their approval—their blessing for the choice she'd made about her path in life.

Knock. Knock.

"Bianca, are you in there?" It was her brother's voice.

"Yes." She'd been found too soon.

The door creaked open and Enzo's somber face met hers. Thankfully, he didn't ask what she was doing in their parents' room. She didn't want to explain how she was grasping at anything that would make her feel close to them once more.

"Everyone is waiting for us downstairs in father's study."

The moment was at hand. Her parents' final wishes would be known. And then the estate would be divvied up between her, her older brother and her younger sister. It would be so—so final. Her parents' absence from their lives would be undeniable.

"I… I'll be there." She turned her back to him, not wanting him to see the unshed tears shimmering in her eyes. She could be strong like him. She could get through this agonizing day without crumbling into a million pieces.

She needed to think about anything but the hollow spot in her heart. She lifted her head and her gaze came to land on the old photos on the wall. It was a collage of her grandparents, her parents' wedding and herself and her two siblings. They'd all looked so happy—

"Bianca, they loved you." And then her brother exited the room, closing the door softly.

It was like her brother to cut through everything to get to the heart of the problem. Did her parents love her like they'd loved her siblings? She had her doubts.

Bianca paused next to her mother's nightstand. It was there that she noticed her mother's journal. She recalled coming across it as a child and her mother shooing her away. She'd asked her mother what she wrote in her journal and her mother said it was a way to vent or a chance to mark something memorable. Her mother didn't write in it often. Her mother had said she liked to reflect upon where she'd come from, so she knew where she was going.

As a teenager, Bianca had tried keeping a journal of her own, but with two nosey siblings close to her own age, it didn't go well. And when her little sister announced one evening at dinner that Alfio Costa had kissed Bianca after school, she had burned her journal and vowed never to write in one again.

She so desperately longed to hear the gentle lilt of her mother's voice but she couldn't recall it. It was like her mind had erased the memory. How could that be? If she was already forgetting her mother's voice, how soon until she forgot what she looked like and their moments together?

She knew that she was being overly dramatic, but her emotions at the moment felt amplified. She didn't know how to calm them. She picked up her mother's journal. Her fingers traced over the buttery soft binding. Inside were her mother's final words.

Her fingertip traced down over the gold gilded pages. Part of her wanted to open the cover and let her mother's voice speak to her. And another part of her said not to do it. Whatever was written within those pages was none of her business. The struggle raged within her.

At last, she convinced herself a fair compromise was just to read a little bit. Just enough to hear her mother's voice once more. One page. That was all. And then she'd put it away.

She let the book fall open to a random page. There was her mother's very distinctive handwriting. Bianca would recognize it anywhere.

Her gaze hungrily took in every word. Once more, she could hear the lilt of her mother's voice. It was as though she were there in the room with her. Her mother was speaking about her upcoming wedding anniversary. There was mention of a gap growing between Bianca's parents and how her mother wanted to do something that would draw them back together again.

Bianca read the last lines of the page.

Has the past come back to haunt us? Has he truly forgiven me? Or does he blame me and my child...

Blame her? And one of her children? For what?

Not even pausing to consider the right and the wrong of it, Bianca flipped the page.

...for the affair.

Bianca's breath lodged in her throat. Her mother had had an affair? How could that be? Her parents always seemed so much in love. How could this have happened?

Bianca dropped onto the edge of the bed, her legs no longer able to hold her up. Her mind grappled to understand the ramifications of this.

Knock. Knock.

The door opened and her younger sister stepped inside. “Hey, Enzo said you were up here. Everyone is waiting for you. The attorney is looking a bit impatient…okay, a lot impatient.”

Bianca didn’t care about the attorney. This news altered everything she thought she knew about her parents—everything she believed about them—everything about her not living up to their expectations.

“Bianca, what is it?” Her sister moved across the room, stopping in front of her. “I know this is hard for you. It’s hard on all of us—”

“It’s not that.” She didn’t know if she should say something to her sister about the affair. Maybe it was best she just left it alone. Was that even possible? This was a bombshell. And it would blow apart her family—

“Hey,” Gia grabbed the journal out of her hands, “this is Mamma’s journal. What are you doing with it?”

Guilt washed over Bianca. “I… I just needed to hear her voice—to feel like she was still here.”

“And so you thought you’d read her private thoughts.”

"It was only one page and then..." Bianca stopped herself. Should she share what she'd learned? How could she not? This changed everything.

"And then what?"

Bianca shook her head. She didn't want her sister to endure further pain. "Nothing."

Her sister studied her for a moment. "It was something all right." Gia lifted the still open journal and read the page. By the bottom line, her mouth gaped and her eyes were rounded. "Seriously?"

Bianca shrugged her shoulders. She wasn't sure what to say. At least she wasn't the only one who didn't know about this affair.

Knock. Knock.

Enzo opened the door. "What's going on with you two? Everyone is waiting downstairs for us?"

Gia motioned for him to come in. "Close the door."

He did as she asked. When he stopped in front of them, he asked, "Why are you reading Mamma's journal? You need to put it back. It's none of your business."

When he went to reach for the journal, Gia was too fast for him. She leaned back on the bed, out of his reach.

Bianca spoke up. "It was only going to be one page. Just enough to feel like Mamma wasn't totally gone. And then—"

"Then we discovered something. Something big."

Enzo shook his head. "Whatever it is. It's none of our business."

"Did you know Mamma had an affair?" Gia blurted out.

"What? No. That can't be right. She wouldn't do something like that." He shook his head as though to chase away the troubling thought. He stepped back from them, distancing himself from the world-shattering news.

Gia scooted back on the big bed, crossed her legs and focused on the journal. She started to read their mother's troubling words. Bianca's gaze stayed on her brother, watching him as the wave of emotions washed over him. It was obvious that he hadn't known about this affair. And the journal didn't say when it'd taken place.

Gia turned the page.

He said that he still loved me and forgave me for what happened, but when we fight, when the distance looms between us, I wonder if he remembers that bad time in our marriage when we separated.

I was so sure that he was never coming back. That we would end up divorced. Days turned to weeks and then to months. I was weak and let a handsome man sweet-talk me into his bed. I've never regretted anything so much in my life. And then the worst happened...

"Stop," Enzo said. "This is wrong."

"I can't stop," Gia said. "This affects us all."

Enzo shook his head. "I don't want to know." Then his gaze narrowed and his voice shook with anger. "Isn't it enough that we lost both of them? Do we have to do this today?"

He might not need to know but Bianca couldn't live with the not knowing. What could be worse than her mother cheating on her father? Bianca needed answers as much as she needed oxygen.

As her sister argued with their brother, Bianca grabbed the journal from her. Her siblings' voices faded into the background as she took in her mother's words.

And then the worst happened. I became pregnant. Aldo said he'd forgiven me and would accept the baby as his own...

Wait. What? One of the three siblings wasn't a true Bartolini? Bianca's gaze hungrily sought out the next words, anxious to know that the family she'd known all her life was truly hers—that she wasn't an outsider.

...but now I wonder if he meant it or if he just accepted the baby because our fami-

lies were pressuring both of us to get back together.

Am I overthinking his words? Maybe he just spoke in the heat of the moment. Tonight, when he comes in from the vineyard, we'll talk. It's the only way to fix things.

Who? Who isn't a Bartolini? Frustration, anger and sorrow churned in her stomach, making her nauseated. The journal was jerked out of her grasp before she could turn the page.

Enzo held the journal. Anger sparked in his eyes. "Stop! We're not doing this. We have a will to read. We have our parents to mourn. The past must stay in the past."

"What are you going to do with the journal?" Gia asked.

"I'm taking it downstairs and burning it in the fireplace—"

"No." Bianca jumped off the bed. "You can't do that."

"Why not?"

"Because one of us isn't a Bartolini. And that's the only key to the past."

CHAPTER ONE

Six weeks later, Bartolini Villa

HE NEEDED THIS EXCURSION.

He wished it could last longer—much longer.

Crown Prince Leopold stood in the lush garden of an Italian villa. He was surrounded by a group of lavishly dressed people. They all wanted a word with him. Why did he think coming to Tuscany would be any different than attending a social occasion in his homeland?

But in that moment, everyone's attention gravitated from him to a woman who'd joined their group. Her bold makeup and flamboyant hot pink outfit matched her personality. He was grateful the woman enjoyed being the center of attention. All he wanted to be was just another person in the crowd. What was it about people always wanting what they didn't have?

Just as his sister, the Princess of Patazonia, wanted a wedding that reflected her personality instead of a traditional royal wedding. But the queen insisted that tradition must rule above all else. Just as his father had said to him, right before he died:

Traditions are the bedrock of this kingdom.

Leo gave himself a mental shake. Now wasn't the time to get caught in the past—in the regrets—in the what-ifs.

Right now, he had his hands full with his feuding mother and sister. The battles between the two headstrong women was a daily occurrence. So when he was invited to this wedding of a childhood friend, he'd ordered up the family jet. Since he was of no help back at the palace, he figured he might as well wish his friend the very best.

Leo moved away from the flamboyant woman. He could take her high pitched, nasally voice only in small doses. Truth be told, there was another woman that had caught his attention. Her hair was dark and her skin glowed a warm tan. He noticed that she spoke when addressed but for the most part she was quiet. And when she did speak, her voice was soft.

He caught himself staring at her more than once. Maybe it was because she didn't make a point of walking up to him and introducing herself like so many of the other people. In fact, she acted as though she didn't even know he was royalty. Could that be possible?

Regardless, his interest in the beautiful woman increased. It'd been a while since he'd enjoyed a woman's company. With his pending engagement and marriage—a necessity in order to ascend to the throne—he wasn't in a position to start anything. But for the moment, he was still a free man.

He noticed how the other men stared at this woman—even the men that were in committed relationships discreetly turned their heads when she walked by. He couldn't blame them. She was stunning. He had to know more about her.

Noticing that she didn't have anything to drink, he snagged two flutes of champagne. He weaved his way through the crowd, dodging attempts at conversation, on his mission to meet the mystery woman. She was difficult to catch up with as she didn't stop to talk to any person for more than a second or two.

At last, he came up behind her. "Excuse me. I believe this is yours."

The woman turned to him. He held the glass out to her. Her brown eyes were filled with confusion. "But I didn't have any champagne."

"I noticed. That's why I retrieved this for you."

She accepted the glass, but he noticed she didn't drink any of it. "Are you enjoying the wedding?"

"I am. The setting is well done. And the gelato treats are unique."

"That was the bride's idea to help keep guests cool."

"You know her—the bride that is?"

"I do now."

"Ah, so you're a friend of the groom."

"I am now." She smiled.

He was confused. Was this beautiful woman some sort of wedding crasher? Was that why she was quiet? He quickly dismissed the idea. There was nothing about her that said she was anything but cultured.

"I'm confused," he said. "Are you a guest of the bride or the groom?"

"Neither. I'm their wedding planner, Bianca Bartolini."

He hadn't expected that response. He must be slipping. He was usually very good at reading people. It probably had something to do with the turmoil back at the palace. By the time he turned in at day's end, he usually had a headache that kept him up until late into the night.

He needed to do something to bring peace back to the palace. If he couldn't do that for his family, how would he ever keep peace over the nation?

He turned his attention back to his beautiful acquaintance. "It's a pleasure to meet you. I'm Pr…erm… Leo."

"It's an honor to meet you."

"You've done a lovely job with the wedding. The groom seems quite pleased."

"Thankfully."

He hesitated. "You say that like there was a chance he wouldn't be happy."

"I only had six weeks to plan this wedding. Six weeks. Do you know how short that is in wedding time?"

Before he could reply, Bianca was called away by the waitstaff. With a curtsy and an apology, she was gone and he found himself disappointed to see her go.

A prince.

A real live, sexy-as-sin, bona fide prince.

And he'd been talking to her. Her heart fluttered. It was all Bianca could do not to spill the drink he'd so kindly gotten for her. But she didn't dare drink it. She had to maintain all her senses throughout the ceremony and reception. Everything had to go perfectly. Her future was riding on it.

Still, no one, including the bride and groom, had told her that the prince, whose face graced every gossip magazine, would be in attendance. Someone should have told her. She would have gone to great pains to make sure he had everything he needed.

Instead she'd stood there trying to keep her knees from shaking. And she had absolutely no idea what she'd said to him. She'd been so nervous. She'd probably made a complete fool of herself. And that curtsy. Did people still curtsy to royalty? She wasn't up on her royal etiquette.

Her rambling thoughts and precious memories of meeting the dashing prince would have to wait until later. Right now, she had a job to do.

She approached the bride, who was waiting to

walk down the aisle. "Camilla, is everything all right? What do you need?"

Camilla looked flustered. "I forgot my gift for the groom." She paced around the study. "I don't know how I could forget the watch. It took forever to pick out the right one. And I had it engraved."

"Don't worry. Everything is going to be all right."

The bride's eyes shimmered with unshed tears. "No. It's not. This is an omen. Our marriage is doomed."

Bianca reached out, taking the bride's ice-cold hands in her own. "I just need you to breathe. Can you do that?"

"But—"

"No but's. Just breathe. Inhale. Deeply." Bianca demonstrated, hoping the bride would follow her example.

Camilla nodded. Her chest visibly expanded.

"And now breathe out." When the bride did as instructed, Bianca said, "Again."

Once the bride was looking a bit calmer, Bianca said, "You keep taking those deep breaths, and I'll be right back. This is all going to work out. I promise."

Bianca let go of the bride's hands and rushed out of the study, closing the door behind her. The ceremony was already a few minutes late. She walked calmly outside to the string octet and asked them to keep playing, entertaining the guests.

As she headed inside, her brother caught up with her. “What’s wrong? Does the bride have cold feet?”

“No.” Bianca said it firmly. “I just have to take care of one thing.”

She dashed past her brother and headed up the stairs to the second floor. Her high heels didn’t slow her down as she headed for the bridal suite. Bianca was certain everything would be all right. This was far from her first wedding—but it was her first wedding all on her own.

Using a master key that each of the Bartolini siblings had, she let herself into the bride’s room. The bed was unmade, pillows were tossed about and there were heaps of clothes strewn everywhere. She’d known three-year-old’s who kept their rooms tidier. She’d send one of the staff up here to tidy things up before the couple turned in for the night.

It took Bianca longer than she’d have liked to locate the bride’s luggage. She searched through the carry-on first, knowing the bride wouldn’t want the expensive watch to be far from her during her flight. It was on the third try that she found what she’d come for.

With the watch in hand, she raced out of the room and down the steps. She rushed into the study where Camilla once more looked like she was just about to have a meltdown.

"Here it is." Bianca placed the watch in the bride's hand.

"You found it. But how? Where?"

"None of it matters. All that matters is that your groom is waiting for you. He's starting to wonder if you're going to walk down the aisle."

"Oh, no! Please go reassure him that I want to marry him more than anything in the world."

Bianca didn't want to ask, but she felt obligated. "Are you sure you want to get married? It's okay if you've changed your mind. I know you were worried about omens—"

Camilla brushed aside Bianca's words. "I was just panicking. Everything is right now." She glanced down at the box containing the watch. "Thanks to you."

Bianca pressed a hand to her chest. "Me?"

"Yes. You've done everything to keep this wedding on track even though it was short notice, and I know I haven't been the easiest bride. I just want to thank you."

"You're welcome. And now I just want to get you down the aisle."

The bride smiled and nodded. "Let's do this." When Bianca turned for the door, the bride followed her. "Oh, here." She held out the watch. "Could you put this in our room for later?"

"Certainly." Bianca smiled and took the box. "You're a beautiful bride."

And with that Bianca headed out the door. She

set the watch in a safe spot inside a buffet until she could get to it after the ceremony. And then she rushed out the back where all the wedding guests were looking a bit anxious.

A number of people turned her way as though wondering what she was doing and why the wedding had yet to start. The groom paced in front of the minister and the groom's younger brother. He stopped when he spotted Bianca.

He rushed up to her. "What's going on? Where's Camilla?"

"Don't worry. She'd misplaced something. But it's been located and now the bride is ready. Shall I have the orchestra play the wedding march?"

"Yes, please. I was so worried she'd changed her mind."

Bianca reached out and squeezed his forearm. "She loves you with all of her heart."

"Thanks."

As Bianca turned away, her gaze caught that of the prince's. He didn't make any pretense to act as though he wasn't watching her. His stare was direct and observant. It made her heart skip a beat.

But she couldn't stop now and talk to him—as much as she wanted. She moved to the orchestra and the wedding music started. Bianca moved toward the French doors that were now open. This was where the bride was to make her grand entrance. The bride's father was standing outside waiting to escort his daughter down the aisle.

When Bianca saw the bride make her entrance, she backed away. She was no longer needed. All her work was done. Now she could take a seat at the back and watch the nuptials. It didn't matter how many weddings she attended, they never became any less romantic.

And it helped that the prince was in her line of sight. She was drawn to him. His bronze skin, dark hair and mysterious eyes were so attractive. A soft sigh passed her lips. If only she could get to know him. But that would never happen.

CHAPTER TWO

WEDDINGS WERE NOT his favorite events.

But Prince Leo had to admit, if only to himself, that the element of *will-they-or-won't-they?* made this particular wedding interesting. He had been leaning toward *they won't*. And by the worried look that had been on the groom's face, he had been leaning the same way.

And then the calm and unflappable wedding planner had made her entrance. She'd spoken softly to the groom and immediately put him at ease. Leo couldn't help but watch her as she took control of the situation. Her demeanor was casual. If she'd been worried about this event reaching its happy conclusion, she hadn't let on.

When he had to get married, he'd want someone like her to organize it. She seemed to roll with the punches as though she'd been through it a million times and knew that all would work out in the end. His sister probably wished she had a wedding planner like Miss Bartolini too.

Right now, the woman organizing the wedding was the same one who had planned his parents' wedding. His sister had tried bringing in her own wedding planner from the nation's capital, but the woman had caved when opposed by the queen and her crony. So his sister's most important day was about to be his mother's vision of how things should be without the bride's input. Leo had tried to help, but he'd been at a disadvantage, not knowing anything about weddings.

He'd known most of his life that when he married, it would be an arranged marriage—a logical, beneficial union. The fact that his parents had planned to have him betrothed as a teenager still soured his stomach. It'd been the last thing he fought about with his father before he'd died suddenly.

It'd taken Leo years to accept that he would marry and have children with a woman he did not love. And so he'd told himself that when he married, it wasn't going to be a big deal to him. It would be done out of duty and obligation—one more thing to tick off the royal duty list.

Love was intended for other people, like his sister. Giselle had found the love of her life and Leo couldn't be happier for her. And that was why her wedding was so important to him. One of them deserved to be truly happy.

"Looks like you have the weight of the world on your shoulders."

Leo turned to find the groom at his side. He smiled, happy for his childhood friend. "Not the entire world, just the weight of Patazonia."

Benito arched a brow. "Problems at home? I hadn't heard anything."

"Oh. You will. Pretty soon my mother and sister are going to have a nuclear meltdown over the upcoming wedding."

Benito laughed. "I can see that happening. Those are two really strong-minded women. You have my sympathies. I'm lucky. Even though our wedding was spontaneous, we had the perfect wedding planner. She took on the big things, including Camilla's parents, and let us enjoy our short engagement. Maybe you should hire her."

Leo was about to dismiss the idea when he realized this might actually work. "You were that impressed by this woman?"

Benito nodded. "Bianca is amazing. She interned with one of the greatest wedding planners in Venice. And now she has returned to her childhood home to start up her own wedding business."

His friend wasn't one to say things he didn't mean. So for him to speak so highly of this Bianca, it meant a lot. If he were to consider hiring her for his sister's wedding, she would report to him. He would at last have some control over this event that was spiraling out of control—and causing a rift between the bride and groom. Best of all, Miss Bartolini wouldn't be a subject of the queen. Therefore, she wouldn't be under her thumb.

The more he thought about hiring his sister a wedding planner, the more he warmed to the idea.

And the fact that Bianca was beautiful as well as composed was just a bonus.

"Have you met her?" Benito asked.

Before Leo could respond, Benito was off seeking out the woman who just might be the answer to his problems. The woman who might bring peace back to the nation. And quiet the gossip floating through the media of unrest in the royal household.

And with that in mind, he didn't try to stop his friend. He was looking forward to doing business with the wedding planner. If this all worked out, he could get back to his search for a bride. And soon he would become king.

A contest.

Not just any contest but one that pitted sibling against sibling.

Bianca still couldn't believe her parents' will had spelled out a competition between her and her siblings to decide who would end up inheriting the vast Bartolini estate. It included the villa, the vineyard, the stables with its award-winning stallions and mares as well as hundreds of fertile acres. It was a paradise of luxury and tranquility.

The siblings who didn't win the contest would lose their childhood home in exchange for an equivalent amount of investments and cash. The money didn't interest Bianca. It was cold and impersonal.

All three of the Bartolini siblings had been raised to appreciate the beauty of this land. And within the walls of this vast villa were all of their childhood memories. And for Bianca, it was crucial to succeed and win this contest.

For it was here in the lush, rolling hills of Tuscany that she intended to establish a destination wedding-planning service. And she was off to a mighty fine start.

Bianca glanced around at the mingling guests. And there was her brother, all dressed up in his finest suit and tie. He definitely didn't look like he spent his days out in the fields tending to the grape vines. In actuality, he cleaned up really well.

After the reading of their parents' will, tensions between the normally civil siblings was running high. It took a bit but the siblings all agreed that they would go with their strengths. Gia would run the boutique hotel, aka their family's sprawling villa. Enzo would oversee the vineyard with its world-renowned Chianti wine. And Bianca had agreed to coordinate weddings at the villa—talk about a romantic backdrop.

An outside accounting firm would be hired to tally their net incomes. Everything was to be aboveboard. And the family's attorney would oversee the contest. Nothing would be left to question. Everything would be certified and final. It seemed so cold—so final.

Enzo smiled at the beautiful young woman next

to him. It was then that Bianca realized it was the first time she'd seen Enzo smile since the journal with their parents' devastating secret had been discovered. It had rocked the very foundation of this family—leaving their relationships vulnerable and strained.

Her gaze moved across the garden area, searching for her sister. Gia hadn't wanted to attend the wedding even though she managed the hotel. Bianca had pushed until she'd agreed. Bianca wanted the Bartolini estate well represented to the influential guest list. She was hoping for new clients—for all of them.

All her life she'd felt as though she didn't fit in. She was different than her siblings. While her brother and sister had enjoyed horses and grapes, she enjoyed the finer things in life. Her father used to get aggravated with her reluctance to get dirty.

And when she was pushed out of the nest, just like her siblings, so they could go off and seek their own path in life, she'd ended up in the UK where she'd worked her way through school. Once her education was completed, she moved to Venice. It was there that she followed her passion with a career in wedding planning. And when she landed a prestigious position as assistant to a world-renowned wedding planner, she thought her wishes had come true.

At first, that had been the case. Things went amazingly well. It was later, when Bianca was ready to put what she'd learned into practice that she realized she was terrible at following directions exactly as they'd been told to her.

She had a penchant for embellishing and taking the bride's ideas into consideration instead of convincing the bride that the wedding planner's methods were the best. Her mentor couldn't deny that Bianca had a flair for wedding planning, even if it wasn't quite the way she'd been instructed.

But now as the bride and groom were surrounded by their guests enjoying the afterglow of the ceremony, Bianca was able to take her first easy breath. Striking out on her own had been the right decision. Things were looking up—

"Bianca, there you are." Benito rushed up to her. "I've been looking everywhere for you."

Immediately she assumed her wedding planner persona. She stood a little taller and straightened her shoulders, prepared to deal with the latest developments. "What's wrong? Whatever it is, we'll deal with it."

Benito shook his head and smiled. "Nothing is wrong. In fact, something is right. Come with me."

He motioned for her to follow and then began walking away without any further explanation. She fell in step behind him, wondering what the normally quiet groom had on his mind.

When he stopped, she stepped up next to him. Her gaze met that of the man standing across from them, Prince Leopold. His eyes were a warm golden-brown that made her empty stomach suddenly feel as though a swarm of butterflies had invaded it.

She didn't know how long she stood there, caught up in his gaze. But when Benito cleared his throat, breaking the connection, heat swirled in her chest, rushing up her neck and setting her cheeks ablaze.

"Bianca Bartolini, I'd like to introduce you to His Royal Highness, Crown Prince Leopold of Patazonia."

Once again, Bianca curtsied. She willed her face to cool down, but it only succeeded in making her warmer. Goodness. What was he going to think of her? First, she was openly staring at him. And now her face must look like a roasted beet—all red and steamy. Not good. Not good at all.

"You've put on a splendid wedding," the prince said. "I've quite enjoyed it."

"Th…thank you, Your Highness."

"The prince is searching for a wedding planner," Benito said. "And I was telling him what a great job you did with our wedding."

"You did?" Then catching herself, she said, "I mean, thank you." She'd wondered after the wristwatch delay if Benito would still be happy with her services. "I'm sorry for the slight delay."

"Don't worry about it. Camilla told me what

happened. Thank you for helping her and calming her down."

Bianca's eyes widened. "She told you all of that?"

"She did. I told her that she just wanted to keep me guessing for as long as she could."

Bianca wasn't used to brides standing up for her. Usually she took the blame, even for something that she had no control over. And when something stunning happened, the bride would take the credit. But every once in a while there were brides that were considerate and kind. Camilla was both of those.

"Anyway, Prince Leopold might be in need of your services. I'll let you two talk." And with that Benito made his way toward his bride.

Bianca's gaze moved to the prince. Her mouth suddenly went dry and she wasn't sure what to say.

What does one say to royalty? Hi? How are you? Beautiful day?

A nervous giggle welled up within her. She stifled it. What was wrong with her? She wasn't the nervous type. She'd worked with the very rich and the very famous. In the end, they were all just people. As her mother used to say, they put their pants on one leg at a time, just like everyone else.

But this man standing before her was most definitely not just another person. When he stared at her, like he was doing now, her pulse raced. Her insides shivered with a nervous energy. Her whole body reacted in the most unnerving ways.

She attempted to compartmentalize all these new and exciting sensations.

Focus on business.

If he had a job for her, it must be something big, something important. And it might be what she needed to launch a successful wedding business.

Coming to her senses, Bianca said, "If I may be of service to you, Your Highness, please let me know."

"There's going to be a wedding. And I think you might be just the right person to help plan it."

He wants me to plan his wedding? Me...planning a prince's wedding?

The honor of such a position was quite apparent to her. To plan such a wedding would mean she would have her choice of weddings going forward. She wouldn't have to search for prestigious clients, they would seek her out.

It would be sad that such a handsome and intriguing man would soon be off the market—not that she was in any position to be courted by anyone—most especially not a prince. With her heredity in question, it was best to keep to herself. But it didn't hurt to daydream.

"Um…thank you, Your Highness. I'm honored to be considered for such a role. Please let me know what I can do to help you."

He didn't say anything for a moment. "Do you have references?"

She nodded. "I can forward them to you."

"I will need to know more about you before I hire you for this very important position."

"Understood."

His expression gave nothing away. "How old are you?"

"Twenty-nine." What did that have to do with anything? But she didn't know the ways of the royals so she kept her questions to herself.

His dark brows drew together as he studied her. "Do you have much experience?"

"I've been working in the wedding industry since I was eighteen."

A brief flicker of skepticism showed in his eyes but in a blink, it was gone. "That's mighty young."

She nodded. "I started interning with a wedding planner when I was at university. My parents didn't believe in coddling their children. When my siblings and I became adults, we were expected to find our own way."

"But this estate is your family's, is it not?"

"It is. But our parents wanted us to rely on ourselves and not our birthright. Even now..." She stopped herself. The wound of her parents' deaths was still too new—too raw—to discuss, not even to gain the wedding of a lifetime.

"Interesting." He held out his hand. "May I have your phone."

She pulled it from the hidden pocket in the folds of her blue satin skirt. When she handed it over, their fingers touched. A tingly sensation raced up her arm and settled in her chest, setting her heart aflutter.

He took her phone and ran his finger over the touch screen. "I have given you my contact information. I trust that you will not share it with anyone."

"You have my word."

He nodded and then returned the phone to her. "Very good. Forward me your references as soon as possible."

She took her phone and moved her fingers over the same touch screen where his long, lean fingers had just been. And in no time, she had completed her task.

His phone chimed and he withdrew it from his pocket. She subdued a smile when his eyes widened as he read his phone. "You have forwarded me the information already?"

She nodded. "I like to be prepared. I keep relevant information on a cloud account."

"Thank you. I will be in touch." And then he turned and walked away.

She wanted to rush after him and ask when he would be in touch. This week? This month? This year? How was she supposed to plan anything when there was a real possibility of working for the Prince of Patazonia?

Or was it nothing more than a fantasy? Would a prince who could hire the best of the best want to hire a no-name like herself? Sure, she'd worked on the biggest and best weddings, but it hadn't been her name associated with those weddings, it had been her boss's. Bianca was still working to make her name known in the wedding world. So thinking a prince would hire her, well, it was nothing more than a fairy tale.

CHAPTER THREE

HE LIKED HER.

He liked her style. He liked her lack of pushiness. He liked her confidence.

And most of all, he liked the thought of her bringing peace to his home.

As the wedding reception wound down, Leo decided to make his move. His assistant had run a preliminary background check on Miss Bianca Bartolini and as for the references, each and every person had nothing but glowing compliments for Bianca and her capabilities.

He'd been observing Bianca. She was not a loud woman, not by any stretch. When the buffet table had run out of pastries, she'd quietly reminded the young woman to refill the tray. No matter what came up, she was on top of it. And had he not been keenly observing her, he wouldn't have noticed that she was constantly working to make the event seamless.

And now he was armed with the information he needed to put his plan into action. He approached Bianca, who currently had her back to him. It gave him a moment to notice the gentle curls of her dark hair with its half up and half down hairdo. The curls settled on the exposed nape of her neck before falling partway down her back. Her narrow waist was accentuated by the sash of her dress.

He followed the dress down over the curve of her hips to where the hemline stopped just a couple inches above her knees. He shouldn't be checking her out, especially not when he was about to hire her. Still, his gaze did its own thing, continuing to the end, where he found she wore a pair of silver stiletto heels.

She was a knockout. So much different from the very prim, very proper wedding planner that his mother preferred to work with. But if he was about to become king, then it was time everyone in the kingdom, including his mother, learned that traditions have their time and place but the future of their nation relied upon their ability to stay current and evolve with the times in order to remain relevant. And Miss Bartolini was going to be his first statement to his mother and the staff.

Next, he'd have to announce his choice for a bride. And he didn't have much time to make this monumental decision. By the end of the year, he would be married. The happily part was doubtful.

The ridiculous requirement in the country's charter about him being married in order to become ruler—talk about your archaic notions. Try as he might to get around that sticking point, it was law. One of his ancestors had written it into the country's charter and now he must abide by it, if he were to step up and be the king that people needed. It was something he intended to change once he was king.

Though he'd dragged his feet about taking on the position, he'd grown a lot in recent years. He'd gotten involved in politics and government, finding that he had a real head for these things. And then he'd gone out in disguise amongst his people and seen how the decisions made by government affected everyday citizens. And he wanted to be a part of that—he wanted to help the people of Patazonia.

But first, he had to see to his sister's happiness.

As though Bianca sensed his presence behind her, she turned. "Your Highness." She dipped her chin. "Is there something I can do for you?"

Just then the orchestra started to play a new song. It'd been a while since he'd danced and from what he'd observed, Bianca hadn't let up on her duties long enough to enjoy the evening. It was wrong for her to miss out on such a marvelous evening.

With the lanterns sending a warm cast over the patio area, he asked, "Would you care to dance?"

Her expressive eyes widened before she resumed her neutral expression. "Thank you. But I shouldn't be seen dancing. I have work to do."

He was surprised by her refusal. He couldn't recall the last time he'd been rebuffed. This just made him all the more determined to get her out on the dance floor.

"You've worked so hard to make this the perfect evening for my friend and his bride. You should take a moment to enjoy the fruits of your labor."

She smiled but didn't say anything.

"Why are you smiling?"

Immediately the smile slipped from her lips. "It's just the way you say some things. It's different."

"Ah, I see. I was taught by older scholars who believed formal speech is befitting a king. Or a king in the making."

"And what do you believe?"

"I believe a good king can speak any way he wants. It's what's in his heart that matters most. And now that I've indulged your curiosity, it's time you indulge mine as well." He held his arm out to her. "Shall we?"

She glanced around as though checking to see if she was needed. And when there was no one around clamoring for her attention, she placed her hand in the crook of his arm. "Lead the way."

That's exactly what he did. Once among the other couples, he clasped her one hand with his own and wrapped his other arm around her waist. Leaving a modest distance between them, they began dancing.

"It was so nice of you to attend the wedding," Bianca said. "Benito must be a really good friend."

"He's a very old friend. I'm happy he found his soul mate."

Her finely plucked brows lifted, but again she didn't say anything.

He couldn't help but be curious about her reaction. "Are you surprised that I'm happy for the couple?"

She shook her head. "I'm just surprised you believe in soul mates."

Perhaps he should watch his wording with her going forward. He didn't like explaining himself, especially about such a sensitive subject. "I do believe in love and soul mates. I just don't believe everyone has one." He noticed the frown on her face. "Has your heart been broken?"

The thought of it didn't sit well with him. He didn't know how a man lucky enough to win her heart could turn around and break it. If it was him—

He halted his thoughts. He didn't even know where that thought had come from. He wasn't looking for love. He was looking for a princess. They were two mutually exclusive things.

"No, it wasn't my heart. Not directly."

Talk about your cryptic answers. But before he could delve further into the subject, the music ended and a round of applause filled the air.

"If you'll excuse me," Bianca said, "I have things to attend to."

His phone chimed. He didn't have to look at it

to know his car was out front, waiting to escort him to his hotel room in Florence. But he had one more thing to do.

"Bianca, I would like to offer you the job."

Her lush lips gaped. It took her a second to regain her composure. "Really? I mean, that was so fast. Are you sure?"

He smiled at her shocked reaction. "Would you like that I change my mind?"

She shook her head as she smiled. "No, I wouldn't."

"I have some business in Florence. Will you be ready to go in two days' time?"

"Two days? Boy, you don't give a girl much warning, do you?"

He hadn't considered that she might have another wedding. "I could definitely make this worth your time?"

Her eyes were like windows to the wheels turning in her mind. If her request for her services was within reason, he would grant it. And then the wedding planner would be all his for the next seven weeks.

"Where are you going? You can't just leave now."

Bianca stopped packing and turned to her sister who was standing in the doorway. She didn't know why Gia cared if she left. All they'd been doing was fighting. And that broke Bianca's heart.

She was starting to worry that they'd never be a real family again.

"I have to go. It's for the best," Bianca said, calmly and emotionless. Tensions were so high that she didn't know what would set off one of her siblings.

"So that's it," her brother chimed in. "What about the estate?"

Bianca looked at Gia, then at Enzo. "I'm leaving because all of this fighting isn't good for us. It's tearing us apart."

Gia crossed her arms and glared at her sister. "You're bailing on us. And leaving me to fight it out with Enzo."

"That's the reason I'm leaving. I don't want to fight anymore. It's exhausting. And it hurts too much." Bianca placed her makeup bag in her suitcase and then crossed it off her packing list. At this point, she had three suitcases. And, according to her lists, everything she would need was packed. It might look like a lot, but she would be working for a prince and she had no idea what she'd need to wear.

"I agree," Gia said.

Bianca closed her full suitcase and then turned to her sister. "You agree with what? That we shouldn't argue anymore? Or that I should leave?"

Gia sighed. "Really? You honestly think I want you to go?"

Bianca shrugged. "I don't know. So much has

been said. And…and what if I'm not a real Bartolini. What happens then?"

Gia pressed her hands to her hips. "What if I'm not a Bartolini?"

Bianca didn't know what words to say to her sister. She couldn't think of any words that would make this situation any better for any of them. They just had to wait it out.

"We'll know soon." Enzo started to pace.

Her brother was referring to the DNA tests they'd submitted last week. But they'd been warned it would be a while until they heard back. Until then, they would have to find a way to deal with the unknown.

"Not soon enough," Bianca muttered.

Gia stepped up next to her sister. "Don't give up on being a part of this family."

"I won't. You either."

"I won't." And then they hugged. When they pulled back, Gia asked, "Do you want help getting these suitcases downstairs?"

"Sure—"

"Hey." Enzo stopped in front of the window. "There's a car here." His gaze moved to the luggage. "I guess it's for you."

She was having the most trouble with him. Everything she said struck him the wrong way. She hoped the distance would help their relationship.

"Enzo, don't just stand there," Gia said. "Grab a suitcase." She gestured to the largest piece.

He hesitated. Then with a sigh, he did as instructed. On the way downstairs, he said, "I don't think you're doing the right thing."

"You never do." Bianca moved to the front door, stopped and turned to face her siblings.

"I can't believe you're giving up on the estate," Gia said.

"She won't have any worries," Enzo said quickly. "She's working for a prince. She'll be paid a fortune."

Gia's lips formed an O. "I didn't think of that. This DNA stuff has me so distracted."

The thing they didn't know was that she was being paid very little. She'd negotiated for something more important—a national marketing campaign for her destination wedding service.

A heated discussion of the ramifications of Bianca's actions on the contest ensued. Should the money she earned for the royal wedding be counted toward her total? Bianca settled the argument by voluntarily excluding the profit from the royal wedding.

But that wasn't enough to bring peace to the family. The heated debate segued to the subject of whether the sibling without Bartolini blood should inherit. Bianca's stomach turned. She was certain they were talking about her.

It all fit. The way she wasn't like her siblings and taking part in the heritage laid out for them by their parents. She'd always felt like a square peg in a round hole—never measuring up in her parents' eyes and always a mystery to her siblings.

Not able to stand the pain in their eyes, she said, "I can't do this! This fighting, it's not us. We never used to fight."

Her brother and sister looked as though they'd been about to say something, but then lowered their gazes and nodded in agreement. It was then that she felt she had to say something—something important.

"I've got to go," Bianca said, "but before I do, I want you both to know that no matter how this contest turns out or what the DNA says, we're family. We're all the family we have left. And…" Her voice faltered. She wasn't used to talking about her feelings to her siblings. "I love you both."

"Aww…" Gia's eyes misted.

And the next thing she knew Gia pulled both her and a reluctant Enzo into a group hug. The closeness didn't last all that long, but it was enough to assure them that they could face these challenges and get through them together.

When they pulled apart, Bianca regretted having to leave, but she'd already given her word and signed a contract. "I can't miss my flight. But I'll be back soon."

"Aren't you flying on a private jet?" Enzo asked.

"The prince's jet?" Gia's eyes were wide with amazement.

A smiled pulled at Bianca's lips as she nodded. And then she was out the door, promising to keep Gia informed about the upcoming royal wedding.

CHAPTER FOUR

HE'D AGREED.

Inwardly, she squealed with delight.

She'd asked for the moon and she'd been given not only it but the stars too.

Bianca sat in the leather seat of the prince's jet as they neared Patazonia. She couldn't believe she was about to become the prince's wedding planner. He'd still not told her the details of his upcoming nuptials. Since she'd boarded the plane, he'd been busy either on the phone or working with his assistant on what she surmised was a very big export deal.

It gave her time to update her day planner as well as make phone calls. Even if she was out of town, it didn't mean she couldn't book weddings at the Tuscany estate. The truth of the matter was she didn't have any other weddings booked, just a handful of people making inquiries.

The reason she'd landed Camilla and Benito's posh wedding had been a fluke. The original wedding planner was pregnant and when complications ensued, she was ordered on bedrest for the remainder of her pregnancy. And taking an immediate liking to Bianca when their paths had crossed in Venice, she'd recommended her services.

Bianca was anxious to get to work on the royal wedding, but the prince kept putting her off. She'd already made an extensive list of questions for him.

As she stared out the window at a passing white puffy cloud, she recalled their dance at the wedding. There had been some sort of connection between them. She'd felt it in his touch and the way his gaze had lingered on her longer than necessary.

Was it wrong that she wanted the prince to notice her as a woman as well as a wedding planner? After all, she was here to plan his wedding—his wedding. Her shoulders sank. Here she was worrying over a man who was taken. What was wrong with her?

Those moments on the dance floor, they must have all been in her imagination. After all, he was so invested in his wedding that he'd taken it upon himself to go out and find a wedding planner instead of leaving all the details up to the bride.

Just then the pilot came over the intercom to let everyone know they would soon be on the ground of Patazonia. It was a small kingdom just off the French border.

In the time since the prince had proposed the job to her, Bianca had been online researching customs and weddings within this foreign land.

The problem was there wasn't much detailed information about Patazonian matrimonial traditions.

"See anything you like?"

She turned to find prince Leo now in the seat next to hers. "I was thinking the land looks so lush. I'm hoping to have a chance to explore the area just a little." And then realizing how that sounded, she rushed to say, "But not before I have all of the wedding preparations in place. Don't worry. The wedding will be my top priority."

"I have no doubt or I would not have hired you. This wedding must go off without a hitch. I am counting on you."

"And the bride, she'll be meeting with us when we land?" She pulled out her notebook. "I have a whole list of questions for her."

The hint of a smile played at his lips. "I doubt she'll meet us at the airport, but she'll be at the palace."

"Good. Good." Nervous energy flooded Bianca's system. She felt like an athlete preparing for their biggest event. She was ready to spring out of the gate and get as much done as fast as she could—all the while paying attention to the details. Because like it or not, as her mentor used to say, the devil is in the details.

"You seem anxious to get started."

"I am."

"I didn't anticipate you would want to start today after traveling."

"There's no time to waste. The wedding will be here in no time." And she'd never done a royal wedding. It would be daunting compared to the garden wedding where she'd met the prince.

Her stomach churned with nerves. What if she had taken on too big of a task? She should have hired an assistant. Maybe she could hire one in Patazonia. In fact, that might work out better. This person would have a full working knowledge of the local traditions.

"Bianca, is everything all right?" The prince's deep, smooth voice drew her from her thoughts.

"Yes. Why do you ask?"

"You looked worried."

She bestowed upon him her brightest smile. "Not worried at all."

And if he believed that she had a Christmas elf to introduce him to. But she was a professional. She could do this. She kept telling herself that as the plane touched down on the tarmac.

Had he made a mistake?

He didn't care what Bianca said. She was worried.

As a dark sedan moved them from the airport to the palace, Leo couldn't tell what it was about this trip that bothered her. And he had yet to tell her about the tension between his mother and sister. Perhaps he should have, but he hadn't wanted to scare her off. He'd already had all the qualified wedding planners in Patazonia turn him down when they realized the queen already had her own planner.

He needed someone on his sister's side. And Bianca was that person. He was pretty adept at reading people. She may be apprehensive now, but he'd seen her in action. He knew when she was in planner mode that nothing ruffled her.

Maybe he should warn her about the exact details of this wedding. He didn't want her totally blindsided—

"I will need an assistant," Bianca said.

"Don't you already have one?"

Her gaze didn't quite meet his. "I thought by hiring one here, they would be able to help with the local customs."

He had to admit it did make sense. "I'll have my assistant provide you with a list for you to choose from."

"Thank you." She glanced down at her list. "And I assume I'll have an office. I mean I could work out of my room, but that would be crowded and awkward—"

"Yes, I'll see that you have a set of private offices."

Bianca rattled off a couple of other items on her list and he was able to appease her. Nothing she'd asked for had been outrageous or over-the-top and by the time she'd checked off everything on her list, they'd pulled up to the palace. His explanation of how things would work would have to wait.

When he'd spoken to Giselle last, he'd told her he had a big surprise for her. He knew how much his sister loved surprises. Even though she was now in her twenties, she was still the first one up on Christmas morning, eager to find out what was in the garishly wrapped packages under the tree.

When the car pulled to a stop, the doors were opened by the staff. Leo stepped out of the car into the late afternoon sun. It didn't matter how many times he traveled, returning home always felt amazing. This place was in his blood—it was a part of him. He couldn't imagine wanting to live anywhere else.

He rounded the back of the car and stopped next to Bianca as she craned her neck, staring up at the palace. "What do you think?"

She continued to take in the enormity of the very old structure with its detailed stonework and its soaring turrets. He stared up at the palace, trying to see it as she did. The gray stone with the ivy climbing up it against the blue sky with the sun's rays peeking out was portrait worthy. Along the border were flowering shrubs. The fuchsia pink blooms added softness to the hard stone. The grounds were perfectly manicured in distinct designs. This place looked the same as it had when his father was alive. Leo couldn't decide if the lack of change was good or bad.

The enormous wooden doors to the palace swung open. The rest of the staff, in black-and-white formal attire, rushed out to greet them.

Leo stopped just outside the doorway next to one of the maids. "Bianca, this is Zola. She will see to anything you need during your visit."

The young woman briefly curtsied.

"Thank you."

Just then his sister came rushing to the doorway. Her long golden-brown hair fell over her shoulders. Her face lit up at the sight of him. He didn't know whether to be flattered that he was missed or concerned that yet again, something was amiss with the wedding.

"You're home." Giselle hugged him, as was her nature.

When they pulled apart, Leo said, "I wasn't gone that long."

"Long enough." His sister frowned. "You should hear what they want to do for the wedding now—"

"Not now, Giselle." Leo's voice was low but firm. "We have a guest."

It was only then that Giselle's blue gaze met Bianca's. The friendly smile returned to his sister's face. She moved to stand in front of Bianca. "Welcome. Leo didn't say he was bringing home company. He can be forgetful that way."

Forgetful? He took exception to that comment. He had a lot on his mind at the moment. And he didn't want his mother to know about Bianca until he'd had a chance to speak with her.

"It's so nice to meet you." Bianca curtsied. "I can't believe I'm here. This place, it's amazing."

Giselle's smile broadened as she moved next to Leo. "She's marvelous. Where did you find her?"

"At a wedding."

Giselle's brows rose. "Really? And you went there voluntarily?"

Leo shrugged off the question. "I've hired Miss Bartolini to plan the wedding."

"And I'm quite honored," Bianca said, punctuating her words with a smile. "But we don't have much time so if you two could sit down with me and tell me what you have in mind for your big day, we can get started."

"We?" Giselle's fingers moved between her and Leo. Her eyes glittered with amusement. "You think *we* are getting married?"

When Bianca turned a questioning gaze in his direction, Leo cleared his throat. "I suppose I was rather light on the details. My apologies. You will not be planning my wedding. You are here to plan my sister, Giselle's, wedding."

Bianca's gaze moved back and forth between the two siblings. "I… I'm sorry."

"It's okay," Giselle said. "It's like my brother to leave out the most important bits of information."

Then she turned to Leo. "I can't believe you hired a wedding planner. Mother is going to have a fit."

"If you'll let me, I can be a big help to you with planning your big day," Bianca uttered. "I have a lot of experience with big weddings, famous weddings and difficult weddings."

That bit of spunk was why he'd hired her. He just hoped Bianca didn't back down when it came to dealing with his mother. Only time would tell.

Giselle's wary gaze turned to Bianca. "How well do you cope with difficult people?"

"Giselle," Leo said, "let's not scare her off before she's even started."

His sister shrugged. "Fair enough. Bianca, once you're settled, we can go over the plans that have been made so far."

Bianca smiled. "I'll be ready."

"I'll show you to your room," Leo said.

"That's okay. I've got this." Giselle moved to Bianca's side. "It'll give us a chance to get acquainted while you go speak to Mother."

Leo had been looking forward to spending more time with Bianca, but arguing with his sister would only arouse his sister's suspicions about his intentions with Bianca. And that was the very last thing he needed at this point.

He nodded. "I'll see you both at dinner."

His gaze briefly connected with Bianca's. It was long enough for his heart to pick up its pace. They'd been together for hours on the trip here and yet they'd barely had a chance to say more than a few words to each other. He deeply regretted it. And now he had to walk away. Why did dinner have to be so far off?

Disappointment shrouded her in its murky grayness. She really had been hoping to talk to him—to get to know him better. There was an air of mystery that surrounded him.

Prince Leopold was different. And it wasn't just that he was royalty, though that was definitely enough to set him apart from anyone else she'd ever known. But there was this invisible yet impenetrable wall that he kept himself cloaked in at all times, much like a body of armor.

As she watched him walk away, she noticed his broad shoulders were pulled back in a straight line. He held his head high as he took long, sure steps. She couldn't help but wonder about the man behind the facade. He might have all the physical things one could want, plus some, but what had happened to him to keep him segregated from the rest of the world?

Once he was out of sight, it gave her a chance to look around. She wasn't sure what she expected to find inside. It wasn't like she'd ever been in a palace before, but this place, it was enormous. The foyer was larger than the flat she'd had in Venice.

From the gleaming marble floors to the sparkling crystal chandelier, she realized this place was ripped out of the pages of a fairy tale. In that very moment, the enormity of the task before her became crystal clear. Not even the biggest, most star-studded wedding could compare to this affair. Her stomach knotted with nervous tension. This wedding would come with challenges, which she couldn't even comprehend at this point.

But she couldn't let Leo or Giselle see her insecurities. She stilled her rambling thoughts. She focused her gaze on her newest client.

"This way." Giselle's sweet voice drew Bianca from her wandering thoughts.

Bianca glanced around for her luggage but didn't see it.

"Don't worry. Your bags are already in your room. Come on." She headed for the grand staircase in the middle of the great foyer.

As they climbed the staircase with a royal red runner up the center, the princess said, "You must be very good at your job for my brother to hire you."

"I am." The admission might sound like bragging. It wasn't. It was the truth.

Bianca might be a train wreck in other areas of her life, but when it came to planning weddings and looking after the details, she was in her zone. Lists were her friends. Her digital calendar ran her life, from a reminder to get up in the morning to the reminder to wind down for the night.

At the top of the steps, the princess paused and

turned to her. "I don't know if you know this, but my brother does not make spur of the moment decisions often." The princess's expression was quite serious. Her gaze searched Bianca as though hunting for answers to unspoken questions. "When he does, it has to be for a very special reason."

She didn't want Giselle to think ill of her. "I can assure you that I did nothing to sway your brother's decision. I didn't even know of your wedding until he brought it to my attention."

For a long tenuous moment, Giselle didn't react. Then as though mulling over Bianca's response, she smiled. "I'm glad he hired you because this wedding needs help." She turned and began walking once more. "And if my brother believes in your skills, then so will I."

"Thank you. I won't let you down."

Giselle led her down a wide carpeted hallway with so much expensive artwork that it felt as though they were visiting a museum. They stopped before an open door and Giselle turned to her.

"Here we are. Your things should already be in your room."

Bianca glanced in the sunny room. It was no less stunning than the other parts of the palace. "Would you like to come in? We could start going over details for the wedding."

Giselle shook her head. "I have to meet with William, my fiancé. But we can speak after dinner." She turned to walk away but then turned back. "Did my brother tell you about dinner?"

"No." She had to wonder what was special about dinner.

"It's sharply at seven. Don't be late. It will be in the formal dining room and dress appropriately. There will be guests."

She was hoping for something more casual, more conducive to work. But when in the palace, do as they do. "I'll see you then."

"One more thing. Did my brother mention our mother?"

"The queen? No." Bianca had a feeling he'd left a lot out and she couldn't wait to speak with him.

"You should know that my mother has very definite ideas of how the wedding should go."

Bianca relaxed a bit. "Most mothers do."

"But my mother is different. She's used to getting her way. But this is my wedding—my day. I want some say in it."

"I'm sure compromises can be made. I'll do my best to incorporate both of your ideas, if that's what you'd like."

"It is. As long as it's more my ideas and less hers."

Bianca smiled. "I understand. I will keep that in mind."

Just then a phone buzzed, and it wasn't Bianca's.

"That's William." Giselle's face lit up. "I must

go. I'll see you later," she called over her shoulder as she rushed away.

Bianca smiled at the young woman's excitement over seeing her fiancé. A deep, abiding love was something special to witness. And that meant Bianca didn't have time to rest before dinner. She stepped into her spacious room and the first thing to draw her attention was a crystal chandelier. It caught the sun's rays shining in through the French doors and sent a cascade of colors across the walls. She'd never stayed in a place so fancy that chandeliers were placed in bedrooms.

But this was far from a bedroom. The beige-and-cream room had a spacious bed with a quilted velvet headboard and footboard, but it also had a full-size couch, two chairs and a fireplace. Her gaze moved slowly around the room. There was just so much to take in, from the intricacies on the ceiling and wall, all the way down to the oriental rug.

Next to the French doors was a small table and chairs. She had a feeling she would be spending countless hours sitting there strategizing particulars for the wedding. She knew that the prince had assured her of having an office, but her working hours never fit into a normal business day. Ideas would strike at all hours of the day and night. And with the high importance of this wedding, she knew her mind would be on business 24/7.

And then there was the prince. A soft sigh escaped her lips as she pictured him. She definitely wanted to impress him—for more than one reason.

CHAPTER FIVE

"I WON'T STAND for this!"

The queen's harsh words echoed in Leo's mind. He knew she wasn't going to take well to his interference in the royal wedding plans, but it was time his mother realized her time as regent—of steamrolling over everyone—was almost at an end. By the end of the year he would be king.

As his mother glared at him, he couldn't help but wonder if part of her hostility was due to the part he played in his father's death. Ever since that horrific day, his relationship with his mother had been strained.

Or it could be that she resented having to step in as regent. Though if that were the case, why had she given him so much freedom up until now? If it weren't for public pressure, would she have pushed him to marry—to step into his birthright?

He had a lot of questions, but he couldn't bring himself to dredge up the past—the most painful period of his life. Because even though he and his father disagreed on certain things, Leo had looked up to his father like some kids idolized sports figures and actors. His father had been his role model.

"Mother, I know you love Giselle, but if you keep interfering with her wedding, you're going to drive a permanent wedge between the two of you."

The queen's eyes flared with anger. "And you think bringing in some stranger that knows nothing of our customs is the solution?"

"I do." He made sure to keep his voice calm. "Bianca is quite capable—"

"Bianca?" His mother crossed her arms as she continued to frown at him. "You're on a first name basis with this woman?"

There was no point in denying it. "Yes, we are on a first name basis. It is not uncommon to call people by their first names."

"And this woman, is she beautiful?"

His jaw tightened in frustration, but he immediately released the tension. He didn't want his very astute mother to get a whiff of his discomfort. She would take it and turn it on him.

"She's a wedding planner. I did not notice her looks." He was lying, but his mother didn't need to know everything.

The queen arched a penciled brow. "I do not believe you."

"This isn't about me or for that matter Bianca. This is about stopping the fighting between you and Giselle. Her wedding is supposed to be a happy time for her—"

"Her wedding is a duty—an obligation—just

as yours will be. It's about forging an alliance with another country. It's about the future of Patazonia."

Leave it to his mother to remove the emotions and go straight for business. Many outsiders thought being part of the royal family was all about sitting back and letting everyone wait on them. But there were things that an outsider didn't know or stop to consider.

As a prince, he was raised to consider how his choices would affect the future of Patazonia. Everything he did was scrutinized by the press—most of the time their headlines were erroneous. But it didn't diminish his need to make careful decisions.

Just like now when there was a growing divide between the royal family and its citizens. The woman he married needed to bridge the gap between the palace and the commoners. It was imperative.

His mother had picked up right where the king had left off with the old-school philosophies. She preferred to remain on her side of the palace wall and rule while the citizens were to remain disconnected on the other side.

When he became king, things were going to change. He wanted to be a king of the people, not a distant, cold ruler. He could do better. This whole dynasty could step up their game by being more interactive and breaking down some of the traditions that had kept them locked in their ivy tower.

He met his mother's angry gaze. "Does the future of this country include fighting?"

His mother gasped. "We were not fighting. We do not fight."

"Then what would you call the slamming of doors and the yelling that has disrupted the entire household?"

His mother's gaze lowered. "Your sister might have gotten a bit emotional over some points with the wedding."

"Some?"

"She wants to throw away everything traditional. But she's a princess. A princess must adhere to certain protocols."

"And was that how it was for you?"

"I don't know what you mean?" His mother glanced away.

This was his opportunity to ask her a question he'd wondered about for a long time. "Did you love my father? Or was it all about obligation?"

The queen, who always prided herself on maintaining her composure, looked at him slack-jawed. Was what he'd asked really that out of line? He supposed. Still, he needed to know the truth.

"This isn't about me or your father." The queen's voice was strained. Her face had noticeably paled.

"It might not have been but it is now—"

"No. It's not." Her firm tone let him know that he'd most definitely crossed a line. "Mrs. Schmidt knows what's best for your sister's wedding. After all, she's been planning royal weddings for nearly fifty years. She helped plan your father's and mine."

"And therein lies the problem, Mother. Giselle is young and times have changed. She doesn't want the same things that a bride of fifty years ago would want." When his mother went to argue, he held up a hand stopping her. "And, as the soon-to-be king, I believe the bride should have a say in her wedding."

"But she'll ruin everything."

"I highly doubt it. I believe a compromise can be reached, marrying some of the old traditions with some of the current trends. And before you resist, remember your future relationship with your daughter is at stake."

His mother huffed. "You're exaggerating."

"Am I?" He'd soothed his sister's tears. He'd listened to her vent about moving away from Patazonia—away from his mother—and moving to her groom's country. Leo knew it wasn't all talk. There was some serious consideration going on.

His mother didn't speak for a moment. At last he'd gotten through to her. "You really believe she's that upset over this?"

"I do. And you need to be careful how you handle things going forward."

"And you just want me to trust this stranger—this outsider?"

"I do. I think if you give Bianca a chance, you'll like her. She's a people person and well organized. Giselle has already met her and they've hit it off." Now that he was finally getting through to his mother, he didn't want to walk away without an understanding. "So will you give this a chance? Let Bianca try to bring peace to this family?"

His mother stirred her tea and then removed the silver spoon, setting it on the fine bone chine saucer. Even standing halfway across the room, he could see the wheels of her mind turning. This wasn't going to be the easy agreement that he'd been hoping for.

Oh, well. So be it. He'd been negotiating with his mother since his father had died. He told himself it was just training for his future as king.

The queen took a sip of tea. Returning the cup to the saucer, she turned her full attention to him. "I'll give your wedding planner a chance, if you'll do something in return."

And there she went with her negotiations, just as he'd predicted. At this point, he was willing to do most anything for some peace in his own home. And most of all, he wanted his younger sister to have the wedding of her dreams with the man she loved.

But he'd been down this road before. To have a party with his friends after graduation, it had cost him. He'd had to wear a suit and tie all summer as he'd visited country after country throughout Europe as part of a goodwill campaign. He couldn't even imagine what this wedding would cost him.

He stifled the resigned sigh. "What do you want?"

A slight smile lifted the queen's lips ever so briefly. "I want you to announce your engagement the day after your sister's wedding."

The day after? As in just a matter of a couple months? Seven weeks, give or take a day?

Leo swallowed hard. He struggled to maintain his composure. His gaze never wavered from his mother's. He didn't want her to detect any weakness. He knew his engagement must be announced soon if he were to be king by the New Year, but this felt so sudden—so final.

The queen held up a finger. "There's one more caveat."

Acid swirled in the pit of his stomach. "I'm listening."

"If you don't choose an appropriate wife by your sister's reception, I'll choose one for you."

He schooled his features as he'd practiced since he was a child. Because a future king could not be emotional. His tutors had drilled that into him since he was just out of diapers.

He intended to tell his mother that horses would fly before he'd allow her to pick his wife, but instead he uttered, "It's a deal."

That little smile on his mother's face bloomed into a full-fledged grin. She got to her feet and approached him. "This is for the best. You'll see."

He highly doubted it. "And you will play nice with the wedding planner?"

It was his mother's turn to sigh. "I will do my best—"

"Mother?"

Her lips pressed into a firm line. "I will hear her out."

"No." He shook his head. "I will receive regular updates and I'll hear everything. I will also have the final decision on the details of the wedding."

"What?" His mother looked horrified. "But you know nothing about weddings."

"I guess it's my caveat. Now, do we have an agreement?"

"You drive a hard bargain." His mother gave him an appraising look. "You're so much like your father. He would be proud of you."

"No one can ever replace him, but I try to do what I think he'd want of me."

"Like the wedding." The queen glanced away. "He would not approve of the bickering. Therefore, I will agree to your plan. However, you must keep in mind that this will be a state wedding with dignitaries in attendance."

"Yes, Mother. But it's also a personal, deeply touching moment for Giselle."

"Agreed. Since we're speaking of your father,

you should know that he would not approve of you putting off your destiny for so long."

"I know." The weight of her words had been pressing on him for some time. It's why he was willing to go along with his mother's bargain. At least Giselle would end up happy. "I will take the throne by the New Year."

His mother turned back to the table. "I have a list of appropriate women for you to consider for your queen."

He'd already been introduced to some women his mother deemed "appropriate." His mother's ideal woman was quiet, meek and dare he say it—boring. He needed a strong woman who spoke her own mind and had a sense of humor so he wouldn't bore of her too quickly.

Sadly, he'd squandered his time to find a wife on his own terms. Now he was left to choose from his mother's preapproved candidates. And his mother knew she had the upper hand. If he had any doubts, the Cheshire smile on her face said it all.

He needed a bit of time to accept what was about to happen—he was going to marry a woman of his mother's choosing. "I must go check on our guest and make sure she has settled in."

His mother turned back to him. "But I'll see you at dinner?"

"I would not miss the kickoff to your birthday celebrations." This was a milestone for his mother. She would turn sixty and a lengthy celebration would ensue over the next few weeks. "We'll both be there."

"Very well."

And with their agreement in place, he departed. His mother wasn't quite herself. Sure, she was one to cling to traditions, but behind closed doors she normally relaxed a bit. That was not the case lately. This wedding had everyone on edge. He was really hoping Bianca would help bring his family back together again.

Speaking of Bianca, he should check on her before dinner, just to make sure she'd settled in without any problems. At least that's what he told himself. Because the truth was that the flight home hadn't gone the way he'd planned. One problem after another kept creeping up and stealing away his time.

But no more. He took the steps two at a time, anxious to see Bianca once more. He wanted to show her around the palace and help her get her bearings as she launched into the wedding preparations.

He stopped outside her door and knocked. "Bianca? It's Leo."

Nothing.

He should probably just walk away and leave well enough alone, but he couldn't resist trying once more.

This time he knocked harder. Louder. "Bianca?"

With a resigned sigh, he turned toward his own private set of rooms. He'd taken no more than three steps when he heard her door swing open.

"Were you looking for me?"

He turned. "I was."

"Sorry. I was out on the balcony, enjoying what's left of this beautiful day."

He retraced his steps. "Your room, is it to your liking?"

"Yes, it is. I think it's the most beautiful room I've ever stayed in."

"That's good." That's good? Was that the best he could do?

But the thing was that every time he was within Bianca's gravitational pull, it messed with his thinking. His thoughts got tangled and his words seemed to lack substance.

It wasn't like him to be caught up in a beautiful woman. Yes, he'd admired many attractive women and he'd definitely enjoyed their time. But none of them had ever driven him to go out of his way to know more about them.

"I was just working on some preliminary plans for the wedding," Bianca said, interrupting his thoughts. "Well, it's more like a list of questions." Her glittering brown eyes lifted until their gazes met. "Perhaps you'd care to help me."

"Yes." What was he saying? He knew next to nothing about weddings. And that was being generous.

But if this gave him more of an opportunity to spend time with Bianca, then he was all for it. He stepped into the room, closing the door behind him. It was then that he inhaled the gentlest scent of wildflowers. It wasn't the first time he'd come across the unique scent.

As he followed Bianca to the balcony, he realized it was her. She was the one who smelled like sweet blossoms. He didn't think he'd ever come across a field of wildflowers without thinking of her.

When she came to a sudden stop, he nearly ran into her. As it was, his hands reached out for her tiny waist, his fingers wrapping around her so as not to bump her into the table.

She turned in his hands. "Sorry." Their gazes met once more. This time he was holding her and he didn't want to let go.

The breath hitched in his throat. His gaze dipped to her berry-red lips. They looked so full, so succulent. What would she do if he were to draw her to him and pluck a deep, long kiss?

He could have his choice of women. There was even a stack of biographies from available, eager women waiting for him on his desk. So why was he drawn to this quiet wedding planner?

Though Bianca was beautiful with her long loose curls, a golden complexion and dark lashes that framed her eyes, which were the mirrors to her soul, she was not from Patazonia. She was not royal. She was not even the daughter of an influential businessman. In his mother's eyes, Bianca was a nobody.

But to him, she was intriguing. She was tempting. And the more time he spent with her, the more captivated he became.

As though Bianca could read his thoughts, she moved out of his grasp. "I… I meant to offer you some coffee. I just brewed a pot."

He raked his fingers through his hair. A cup of coffee would be good. It would give his hands something to do besides finding their way back to her. Because if he were to pull her close again, he couldn't guarantee that things wouldn't move from a business relationship to something much more intimate.

"That sounds good." He took a seat at the small table on the balcony.

A minute later, Bianca returned with a full cup. "I forgot to ask what you take in your coffee."

"Black is fine." Right now, he wasn't sure he would actually notice what he was drinking. As Bianca took a seat next to him, his full attention returned to her. "How may I help with the wedding?"

She opened her laptop and moved her cursor to the top of a form. "Do you know approximately how many guests to expect?"

While the sun began its slow descent toward the horizon, he answered as many of her questions as he could. He surprised himself by how many details he'd picked up on by listening to his sister and mother argue.

He knew things about his sister's dress. Whether the ceremony would be ultraformal. And he knew where the reception was being held. Even the number of courses to be served for dinner.

"I'd like to do something for my sister on her wedding day," he said. "She's making a lot of concessions to please my mother and go along with tradition, but I think she needs a chance to let down her hair and live it up on her big day. Do you have any ideas?"

Bianca stopped typing and thought for a moment. "Since the wedding is early in the day, you could do an after-party."

"An after-party." He mulled this over. "Does this mean we could have a select list of guests?"

"Certainly. You could exclude some of the guests from the ceremony and include some others that were not fortunate enough to receive a ceremony invite. The after-party can be as formal or informal as you'd like."

This appealed to him. He knew his sister and her fiancé had a lot of friends—friends that had to be overlooked for invitations to the ceremony in order to invite heads of state and dignitaries from all over Europe and beyond. This would be a way for his sister to have everyone she cared about around her on her big day.

"I like it," he said. "But for the moment, let's just keep this between us. I'll have a list of guests for you by the end of the week."

"That's good because we don't have much time to plan something like this." She hesitated.

"What's bothering you?"

Her gaze lifted to meet his. "With it being so close to the wedding, a lot of people might have other obligations already?"

"Let me worry about it. You pick out an appropriate invite and I'll put together the list."

"What about the venue?"

"That's the easiest part. We will have it at the Hampstead estate next to the lake. It's about fifteen kilometers from here. Far enough that it won't bother my mother with the loud music."

Bianca's eyes widened. "You were serious about letting your hair down."

"Definitely. I just wish I'd have thought of it."

"Why? I don't mind sharing ideas with you. After all, it's my job."

He shook his head. "It's not that. If I'd have had this idea a lot sooner, I could have booked some headline bands. As it is, they are probably all booked."

They continued to talk about bands. He named the ones he'd heard his sister mention. Then he inquired about Bianca's favorite band and in turn, he told her his. For a moment, it wasn't work. It was like they were two friends getting to know each other.

"Thank you." Bianca finished her list of potential bands. "I'll do the best I can to get someone your sister will approve of."

"And my mother doesn't need to know about any of this for now. Speaking of which, it is time to dress for dinner." He got to his feet. And then he realized he needed to make something else perfectly clear. "You will be reporting to me on this wedding. I know my mother likes to think she's in control, but I would like to have dinner with you each evening to go over everything—to make sure we're on track."

Bianca nodded. "Understood. And we can discuss my promotional campaign."

He couldn't help but smile. "I won't forget. I already have my people working on some preliminary mockups. I'll have them for you to approve shortly."

Her face lit up with excitement. "Thank you."

"I'll stop back and walk you to dinner." And with that he left.

CHAPTER SIX

IT WASN'T A QUESTION.

It wasn't an invite.

It was a declaration. Prince Leopold would be escorting her to dinner.

As Bianca stared into the mirror, she became distracted. Try as she might, she couldn't forget the turmoil back in Tuscany. Her attention focused on her face. She searched for signs that she was a Bartolini. Her nose—was it too small? She turned this way and that way.

Her eyes—were they too close together? Were they the same size and shape as her father's? She struggled to conjure up the exact details of her father's face. The more she struggled to recall, the more frustrated she became.

As she continued to stare at her reflection, she remembered people commenting on how much she resembled her mother. Was that a clue? Did she look like her mother because her father wasn't truly her father?

And if she wasn't a Bartolini, who was she?

The questions tumbled through her mind. They weighed on her, putting everything she thought she knew about herself into question.

Tears of frustration pricked the backs of her eyes. She blinked repeatedly. How long were those DNA tests going to take? The wait was agonizing.

But right now, she had an important dinner with the royal family. She put on diamond stud earrings followed by diamond dangle earrings. She may be a poor pauper compared to the wealth of this royal family, but back in her own world, the Bartolini's had made a name for themselves.

She gazed down at the navy-and-silver dress she'd selected for this evening. It was formfitting and hugged her curves. As she stared in the mirror, she sucked in her breath, pulling in her stomach. Maybe this wasn't the right dress to wear for meeting the queen for the first time. But when she checked the time, it was a quarter to seven. Too late to change now. She expected Leo to arrive any minute.

Bianca slipped on the silver rhinestone–studded stilettos. Still, she was stuck on the fact that a prince—a sexy, gorgeous prince—would be her escort for dinner. Who cared if he was a bit presumptuous? She knew how to put him in his place if he got obnoxious. Though she just couldn't imagine Leo being an overbearing jerk.

As she finished with the delicate strap on her shoe, her attention focused on her nails. She'd had them done for the wedding at the vineyard. She lifted her hands to her face and inspected them.

Other than a slight tremor, they looked good. The French manicure was holding up nicely. The last thing she wanted was to greet the queen looking anything other than her best.

The nervous tremor that had started in her hands moved to her stomach. She was meeting a queen. Who did that? People with a much higher social status than her. She didn't even know what to say to the woman. Her mouth grew dry. Her brain drew a blank.

Don't think about it. Think about something else.

She wanted someone to share this moment with. Her thoughts turned to her sister. She knew Gia would be in awe over this just as she was. And she had promised to let her siblings know when she'd arrived safely.

She reached for her phone. As she went to pull up her sisters' number, she paused. The last time she'd seen them, there had been a big argument. She didn't want to go there again. Perhaps a text message would be best.

Arrived safely.

Immediately a response pinged on her phone.

Exciting! What's it like?

Amazing!

And the prince?

Bianca thought for a moment. Scads of adjectives raced to the front of her mind.

Amazing!

#jealous Tell me more.

Knock. Knock.
"Coming," Bianca called out.

Can't now. My prince...

Bianca groaned. *Erase. Erase.*

Can't now. The prince has arrived for dinner.

#exciting Don't forget. Details. Lots of details.

LOL. Talk soon.

Bianca smiled as she set aside her phone. Things were starting to seem normal between her and her sister. Perhaps she'd had the right idea about putting a little distance between them. Because during this whole thing of losing her parents and the mess with the will, she could really use her friend—her sister.

Knock. Knock.

"Bianca, are you ready?"

"Yes. I'll be right there." She glanced in the mirror. She adjusted a stray hair and then smoothed the makeup under her left eye. It was as good as it was going to get.

She moved to the door and swung it open. She didn't know it was possible for Leo to look any better than she'd seen him so far. But she'd been wrong.

His short dark hair was still damp from his shower. The sides were clipped close to his head while the curls on top were short but just long enough for them to do their own things. And what they did made Bianca want to reach out and run her fingers through the damp curls.

Her gaze met his smiling eyes. Her heart raced. His face was clean-shaven. She paused to inhale, imagining the slightest hint of a spicy aftershave. Mmm… She longed to take a step forward and lean into him for a real whiff.

"You look beautiful." His voice drew her from her meandering thoughts.

"Th-thank you." She needed to calm herself. Otherwise she was likely to make a fool of herself in front of the queen. If she did that, she'd end up fired before she even began her job. And she didn't want to think of the negative consequences to her business.

"Are you ready to go?"

She glanced back at the room just to make sure

she hadn't forgotten anything. She leveled her shoulders and turned back to him. "I'm ready."

He arched a brow. "Are you sure?"

"Positive."

In true princely fashion, he held his arm out to her. "Then let's go."

She stepped out, pulled the door shut behind her and then placed her hand in the crook of his arm. The heat of his body radiated into her skin, warming her cell by cell, bone by bone. Did he have any idea what he did to her heart rate?

She hoped not. As it was, she had to concentrate on walking. She didn't want to trip over her own two feet. How embarrassing would that be?

She swallowed hard, trying to put on a calm exterior. "What's your mother like?"

"Hmm… How long do you have?"

"Oh, boy."

A soft deep laugh rumbled in his chest. "Relax. I'll be there with you."

That was of little comfort considering she didn't rely on others to fight her battles. It was one of the lessons her father had instilled in her and her siblings. To make it in this world you have to be strong with a kind heart.

"How do I address her?"

"Don't address her unless she speaks to you first. And then you may refer to her as Your Majesty."

"Oh, my. That formal, huh?" This definitely

wasn't like any other time where she'd gone to meet a boyfriend's mother. Far from it.

Leo nodded. "My mother is a stickler for titles, duty and tradition."

"What do you call her?"

"Mother, in private."

"And in public?"

"Your Majesty."

It took a second for Bianca to realize that her mouth was agape. She couldn't even begin to imagine what it was like to grow up the way he had.

Sooner than she was prepared for, they arrived just outside the dining room. Leo turned to her. "Are you ready?"

Bianca nodded.

With her stomach twisted in a nervous knot, she entered. She found Giselle standing by a tall handsome man who must be her fiancé, by the way she was looking at him.

Next to them stood another couple. They were older. The man looked quite distinguished and though he didn't smile that often, his wife beamed as she made small talk with Giselle.

And then Bianca's attention moved to an older woman with silver hair. It was cut short into a neat bob. That she presumed was the queen. Her stomach shivered with anxiety. Surely that queen couldn't be as intimidating as she was imagining. Could she?

Leo came to a stop near the group and waited for a pause in the conversation. "Mother," he waited until she turned her attention to them, "I'd like to introduce Bianca Bartolini of Tuscany, Italy." And then he turned to Bianca. "Bianca, I'd like to introduce the Queen of Patazonia."

Bianca's mouth went dry but her brain worked just enough for her to remember to curtsy to the queen. She hoped that was right. When she straightened, the queen was staring at her with a hawk-like stare. Bianca's breath stilled in her lungs.

She felt so out of place—so out of her realm. But she couldn't falter. She had to stay strong for Leo, for Giselle, for herself. Without this account, the future of her wedding business looked uncertain. She needed her business as her touchstone. Without it she'd be adrift.

Leo had warned her not to speak until spoken too. And yet she felt compelled to say something—anything to break this awkward silence.

"It's so nice to meet you, ma'am. I'm honored to be here. Your palace, it's quite extraordinary."

A penciled brow rose. "Perhaps if my son isn't too busy, he can give you a tour of the gardens before you leave. They were my husband's passion."

"Thank you but..." Just then Leo gave a slight shake of his head. Bianca adjusted what she was about to say. "I will definitely make a point of visiting the gardens."

"Very well. Shall we eat?" The queen started for the head of the table.

The queen acted as though she were there just for the evening. Did the woman not know that she was the wedding planner? Had Leo failed to tell her?

Bianca glanced over at Leo who was making conversation with a gentleman who had such a sour expression that it looked as though he'd just sucked on a lemon. She had no idea who the man was but he obviously didn't have a very optimistic view of life.

Thankfully she'd been seated near Giselle. She really liked the young woman. She was warm and vivacious, unlike her mother. Bianca also noticed that the bride-to-be mentioned the wedding only once in passing. She found that odd. Most of the brides she'd worked with were quite excited for the big day and would talk about the preparations almost nonstop. Perhaps the rift between mother and daughter was the reason for the quietness on the subject.

The queen made a point of talking to each person at the table except Bianca. It was as though she were invisible. It wasn't an ideal way to begin a working relationship, but at least she hadn't been banished. That had to count for something. Right?

When the queen mentioned the gardens once more to her guests, Bianca seized the opportunity. "I'm very anxious to see the gardens. It would be a beautiful backdrop for the wedding. In fact, I just hosted a garden wedding at my family's estate. It's where I met L…erm…the prince."

"Is that so?" The queen turned to her son.

"Yes. I attended Benito's wedding."

"I see. Now I understand why you feel like an expert on the subject."

The seconds ticked away as mother and son stared at each other. A war of wills quietly ensued. Bianca felt bad for Leo. He was only trying to help his sister have a happy wedding. This wasn't his fight but he was taking it on for his sister's sake. Bianca's respect for him escalated.

"I hope to be able to make this wedding a very memorable and happy occasion for everyone," Bianca said, trying to diffuse the situation.

The queen turned to her. "This is not your typical wedding. Giselle is a princess and certain obligations go along with that title—even if she doesn't like it."

She's the mother of the bride. Just the mother of the bride.

Bianca lowered her hand to her lap where no one could see its slight tremble. And then she pasted on a bright smile. "I'm eager to learn of your traditions."

The queen arched a disbelieving brow. "Are you? Because I already have a wedding planner that knows everything about planning a royal wedding."

"And I'm looking forward to working with her. I think we'll be able to make room for your traditions and for Giselle's wishes." Bianca could now understand why Leo had brought in reinforcements. The queen was very determined to have her way, no matter how unhappy it made her daughter.

And that was it. The conversation ended as the queen turned to the female guest to her right.

CHAPTER SEVEN

HER CONCENTRATION WAS AMISS.

It might have something to do with a very handsome prince staring across the table at her.

Every time Bianca's gaze met his, he would glance away. Was it possible the prince was interested in her? Or was it a case of wishful thinking?

She didn't know how she did it, but she made it through the seven-course dinner without spilling her water, dribbling her wine or dropping her fork, even though her hands insisted on trembling. Giselle included her in a friendly conversation, but Leo for the most part was quiet. He paid attention to the conversations around him, but he didn't participate unless someone directly addressed him.

When dinner was concluded, the queen, the prince and Giselle's fiancé spoke with their guests about a matter of government while Giselle pulled Bianca aside. They walked to the terrace, which overlooked the gardens that were highlighted by a vast array of soft lights. They were huge and looked exactly like a maze. Her inner child was anxious to go explore.

"I think you impressed my mother," Giselle

said. "But she would never let on. She isn't used to someone standing up to her."

Bianca worried that she'd said too much. "I hope I didn't offend her. That was not my intention."

"My mother does not respect many people. And certainly not the ones she can easily walk over. That's why my brother is the perfect person to be king. He stands up to our mother and calls her out on things when she goes too far."

"And what about you?" It would be helpful to get more information about the dynamic between the bride and her mother.

Giselle shrugged. "Before the wedding, my mother and I never had much of a reason to clash because I was never interested in the inner workings of the country. There were always enough people handling affairs of state, allowing me to concentrate on my own life. But this wedding, it went from being my marriage to William to being worldwide publicity for our country. There are news networks bidding for strategic camera placements within the cathedral." There was a tone of disbelief and disgust in her voice. "Can you imagine?"

Actually, she could. She once did a wedding for two American movie stars. The paparazzi was everywhere. And the first photo of the newlywed couple sold for millions. But that wouldn't do anything to soothe this bride's nerves.

"I'll handle the press. That's not for you to worry about."

Giselle studied her for a moment as though trying to figure out if she should trust her. "You've dealt with big weddings before?"

"Yes. I've worked for some very famous people. Some of them had huge weddings and others preferred privacy. Every wedding is different. Just as every bride is different."

"My brother must really like you." Giselle smiled like she knew a secret.

Bianca glanced around, afraid someone might overhear them. Luckily there wasn't anyone too close to them. "I think he likes the way I do my job."

Giselle's smile broadened. "He's never brought home a woman before."

Heat engulfed Bianca's face. "It's only work."

"Uh-huh." But the look in Giselle's eyes said that she didn't believe her.

"We're working on your wedding and—" She caught herself, not sure if Leo would mind if she shared their arrangement.

"And what?" Giselle drew out the words with a definite note of interest. "Do tell."

"It's no big deal." That was a lie. It was a huge deal to her. "In exchange for me planning your wedding, he has agreed to sponsor an advertising campaign to draw people to my family's vineyard in Italy for my wedding planning business."

Giselle didn't even attempt to hide her gaping mouth. It took her a couple of seconds to speak. "My brother is doing all of that?"

"Yes. For you. To give you the wedding of your dreams."

"My brother isn't the kind to go out of his way for just anyone. Trust me. He likes you."

"It's not for me. It's for you."

"Uh-huh." Her eyes said that she didn't believe her.

Bianca's stomach fluttered as though it'd been invaded by a swarm of butterflies. Giselle had to be wrong. Leo wasn't interested in her—

"There you are." Leo's voice came from behind them.

Both Bianca and Giselle turned. When Bianca's gaze met his, her heart beat wildly. And this was all Giselle's fault for putting these wildly inappropriate thoughts into her mind.

Giselle glanced around. "Where's William?"

"He's waiting inside for you. Everyone has called it an evening."

Giselle turned to Bianca. "I'm glad you're here. I like you. And I think together, we'll plan a great wedding. Can we meet first thing tomorrow to go over details?"

Bianca nodded. "That would be perfect."

"I'll see you then." Giselle headed back inside. She paused next to her brother. "You have good taste. Just don't go and scare her off."

Leo arched a brow at his sister but didn't say a word. Giselle giggled as she headed inside, leaving them alone in the moonlight.

He approached her. "You did well at dinner. My mother is not an easy woman."

"But I don't think she likes me."

"I'll let you in on a secret—I don't think she likes many people. But give her time. She won't be able to resist liking you."

His words warmed a spot in Bianca's chest. That warmth radiated up her neck and once again set her cheeks ablaze. She wasn't one that normally blushed but there was something about being here—talking with Leo—being so close to him.

"I think you're trying to put me at ease, but I know dealing with your mother over this wedding is not going to be easy. She has her thoughts and they aren't easily going to be swayed, but I intend to do my best. I can at least run interference for your sister. Your mother can yell at me—"

"My mother rarely raises her voice. It's more along the lines of looks that could kill as well as a warning tone in her voice that makes people quiver."

"Quiver, huh? Are you trying to get rid of me?"

"Not a chance. Instead, I came out here to see if you'd like to stroll through the gardens with me." He once again held his arm out to her. "Shall we?"

She loved his gentlemanly ways. The guys she'd

dated didn't do things like offer their arm, get her chair for her or open her car door. But Leo, he was definitely different.

She placed her hand in the crook of his arm and walked with him as they moved to the sweeping stone steps that led to the gardens. As they moved along the cobblestone walkway, she inhaled a sweet floral scent. It was delightful.

"This is beautiful. How big is it?"

"Every year, they expand it. I don't know exactly how big it is. I just know that when I was little, it was fun to play in. But the head gardener wasn't so happy when we veered off the path and trampled the plants."

The thought of Leo as a young boy made her smile. "I bet he wasn't that upset with you."

"Oh, I think he was, but there wasn't much he could do since I was a prince. And so we kept playing out here and getting in more trouble."

"I can't blame you. When I was young, my brother and sister would play with me among the grapevines at the vineyard. But it was nowhere near as fun as this winding garden path. There are so many hiding places."

"There's a lot more to Patazonia than the royal gardens. I hope to show you around while you're here." He stopped and turned to her. "You haven't changed your mind about the wedding, have you?"

She shook her head. With him gazing into her eyes, her heart had leaped into her throat. Was that desire reflected in his eyes? The prince desired her? Her heart tumbled in her chest.

She didn't know how long they stood there staring into each other's eyes. It was like Leo had a gravitational force around him and she was being drawn in. Though she knew letting anything happen between them would be a mistake—compounding all of the other uncertainties in her life—she remained rooted to the spot in front of him.

Her heart raced as she found herself getting lost in his dark gaze. Her fingers tingled with the urge to reach out to him—

Someone cleared their throat. Loudly. Annoyingly.

And in that second, the connection dissipated. Bianca blinked and glanced away. Heat returned to her face. She was grateful she didn't have to speak because she didn't trust her tongue to work correctly.

Leo cleared his throat. "Yes, Michael. What is it?"

"You are needed, sir. The call from Canada."

Leo sighed. "I'll be right there." Once the man moved on, Leo turned his full attention to her. "I'm sorry. I've been expecting this call all day."

"I understand. You have important business to attend to."

Reality had come crashing in on them. And none too soon. He was a royal prince. She was a wedding planner with an uncertain heritage. They did not belong together.

"About this..." As his voice trailed off, he looked at her with confusion reflected in his eyes.

He wasn't the only one to be confused. Her heart had betrayed her mind in wanting what it could not have. And now that her feet were once again planted firmly on the ground, she couldn't forget that she was here to do a job. That needed to be her focus. Not getting swept up in some fairy tale.

"It's okay," she said. "You have important work to do."

"You're not upset about ending the evening so soon?"

She shook her head. "Not at all. I understand that business must come first."

As he escorted her back to the palace, he didn't offer her his arm. And she made sure to keep a reasonable distance between them. Because as much as nothing had happened between them, something most definitely had almost happened.

For a brief moment awareness had passed between them. It had been something genuine. Something not quite tangible but utterly unique. But for both their sakes, it was best neither of them examined it too closely.

CHAPTER EIGHT

HE'D ALMOST KISSED the wedding planner.

And the only thing he regretted was that they'd been interrupted.

A hectic week had flown by since that very memorable moment and Bianca filled every nook and crevice of Leo's thoughts. He sighed. He was playing with fire. He was supposed to be choosing a wife in order to announce his engagement after his sister's wedding, not indulging in a fleeting desire. But, oh, what a desire.

"What are you smiling about?"

Immediately Leo cleared his facial expression. His sister stood in front of his desk studying him. How long had she been there? He'd been so caught up in his thoughts that he hadn't heard her enter his office.

He leaned back in his chair. "Good morning, Giselle."

"From the look on your face you must have had a good night too."

He frowned at her, warning her off the subject. But his sister wasn't good with warnings. She dared to tread where most people would veer away.

"If you must know, I worked late into the night. And it was a very successful meeting."

Giselle crossed her arms. "If that's what you need to tell yourself, then go ahead. But I think it was something far more personal that had you smiling."

He cleared his throat. "Did you need something?"

"You didn't show up at breakfast—"

"I was working."

"And Bianca wondered where you might be."

He leaned forward and straightened the papers on the desk. "I thought you would be working with her this morning and going over all of the relevant details for the wedding."

"We are. I'm just waiting for her to grab her things and then we're off." He could feel her gaze on him the whole time she spoke. "I just stopped by to see if you would want to accompany us."

His gaze moved to the stack of bios of potential wives for him to choose from. He'd been dragging his feet long enough. The time had come. It wasn't just his mother who was pushing for him to move into the role of king. It was the cabinet too. And, truth be told, he'd been allowed his freedom to be young and a bit adventurous. Now, it was time for him to assume his responsibilities. Even if marrying for duty wasn't something he relished.

He stared blindly down at the papers on his

desk. "Thanks. But I have a lot of work to catch up on."

He'd used the excuse of urgent business to cancel his daily meetings with Bianca. Though he really did have pressing matters, he needed the time and distance to regain a certain level of detachment where the alluring wedding planner was concerned.

"You're sure? You and Bianca seem to enjoy each other's company."

His sister was right, but he wasn't going to encourage her. "I'll catch up on the wedding plans this evening."

Now that Bianca had had a chance to settle in, it was time she filled him in on the progress with the wedding. If there were problems, he wanted them addressed straight away. Nothing would ruin this event for his sister.

Giselle turned to leave but then turned back to him. "How did you get Mother to go along with this plan?"

His gaze met hers. "It's not for you to worry about. I told you I would work this out so that you could enjoy your wedding and I've done just that."

Giselle rushed around the desk, wrapped her arms around him and pressed a feathery kiss to his cheek. "You really are a great brother. And someday I'll pay you back for all you've done for me."

"I didn't do it for payback."

Giselle pulled away. "I know. You did it because

you love me." She moved to the other side of the desk. "I'm your favorite sister."

"You're my only sister. Now go before I disown you." He sent her a teasing smile.

She smiled back at him. "I'll tell Bianca you're sorry you were detained, but you're eager to see her this evening—"

"Giselle—"

She scurried out of the office, giggling the whole time.

He shook his head. His sister had a good heart, but she could be relentless at times. He just hoped when he did pick a wife that she would be friends with his sister. It'd be nice to finally have some family harmony.

At last, he'd run out of excuses to resume his search for a wife. As the queen had reminded him that morning in the hallway, only six weeks remained until Giselle's wedding followed by his official engagement announcement. And there was no way he would allow his mother to choose his wife. He inwardly shuddered at the thought.

He reached for the first bio on the rather large stack. As he started to read the page, he found himself comparing the woman to Bianca. He stopped, trying to clear Bianca's beautiful image from his thoughts. He started to read again. This candidate's photo had short hair unlike Bianca's long hair—he stopped again. This was going to take a long, long time.

* * *

Was he avoiding her?

Had that moment of attraction unsettled him?

Those were the questions that snuck into Bianca's thoughts as their dinner meetings had been cancelled night after night. She'd scarcely seen him since that moment in the gardens.

She tried to tell herself that he was a prince and therefore very busy. And that had worked the first day. But she couldn't lie to herself any longer. Leo was avoiding her. It hurt.

And for that reason, Bianca had kept herself busy from first thing in the morning until she'd passed out from utter exhaustion late at night. Planning a national event was not for the faint of heart.

This morning, Giselle was giving her a tour of the cathedral. Its soaring arched roof was jaw-dropping. The stained-glass windows were stunning works of art. And the suspended lanterns were absolutely charming. This church would provide the most stunning backdrop for the wedding. Bianca made a list of items she'd like to address later, after she'd given them some thought.

At lunch in the nearby village, Bianca tried her best to catch everything Giselle said. However, the princess was the opposite of her brother. Where he was reserved and spoke only when he had something substantial to say, Giselle rambled on about this, that and another thing.

The princess was like a sunny ball of energy. And Bianca could easily imagine them being lifelong friends. Not that it was possible. When the wedding was completed, her time in Patazonia would also be completed.

But would Leo avoid her until then?

"What's the matter?" Giselle asked as the chauffeured car whisked them back to the palace earlier than expected.

"Um…nothing." Bianca lied. There was no way she was discussing Leo with his sister. If Giselle didn't approve of the match, she would fire Bianca on the spot. And if she did like them together, she would just make the whole situation even more awkward.

"That frown on your face says you have something on your mind," Giselle said. "You can talk to me."

"I was just thinking about the wedding." She needed a diversion. "You've told me what you want for the wedding and now I have to speak to your mother and her planner to find out what they expect."

"Do you have to?" Giselle's voice carried with it a slight whine.

"My goal is to give you the best day of your life. A day you can look back on and smile. If you're fighting with your mother throughout the whole ordeal, you aren't going to enjoy your big day and you definitely won't want to remember it."

"You're right." Giselle looked down at her skirt and picked a piece of lint from it. "You know, William and I have even talked about eloping. But please don't tell my brother and certainly not my mother. She would explode and then lock me in the tower until the wedding."

"My lips are sealed. But is that what you really want to do?"

Giselle shrugged her slim shoulders. "It's better than fighting about everything, even down to the table linens."

"Then it's a good thing I'm here. You don't have to fight anymore. I'll be your go-between."

"Thank you. I feel so much better with you here." The car pulled to a stop at a side entrance to the palace. "Now, let's get you back to your office."

"That would be nice. I have so much to do."

"And I believe someone will be waiting for you."

Bianca's heart raced with anticipation. She couldn't wait. Her steps were quick through the maze of hallways until Giselle stopped outside the door. "I won't keep you any longer."

"Thank you for everything. I won't let you down."

"I know you won't. I can see why my brother hired you on the spot."

Bianca sent her a reassuring smile. "I'll send you the questionnaire I use for the details of the ceremony. If you could get that back to me right away, it would be helpful."

"I will." Giselle took a few steps down the hallway before pausing and turning back. "You know this is the first time I've been truly excited about the wedding. I just know with you here it's going to be extra special."

Once Giselle was gone, Bianca opened the office door fully expecting to find Leo waiting for her. Instead, standing behind an oversized dark wood desk was a beautiful young woman.

"Hi." The young woman straightened. "You must be Bianca." She moved from behind the desk. "I'm Sylvie. I'm your assistant for the wedding."

The young woman appeared to be about her age and she had the friendliest smile. "It's nice to meet you, Sylvie. Have you ever arranged a wedding before?"

She nodded her head. "I work for a wedding planner in town. The prince—" just the mention of him had the young woman blushing "—hired me to help you."

"I hope he didn't take you away from anything important."

Sylvie vehemently shook her head. And then with a perfectly serious expression, she said, "Nothing could be nearly as important as the royal wedding. I just can't believe I was chosen over all of the other more experienced people."

Bianca couldn't help but smile at Sylvie's sense of awe. "I'll tell you a secret. I was surprised too when the prince hired me."

"You were?"

Bianca nodded. "I've done a lot of big weddings but nothing this big and not on my own."

"You aren't alone. You've got me."

"And together, you and I will give Giselle and her fiancé the wedding of the century."

"Let's do it."

They sat down and went over what Bianca had sorted out so far. They made lists because nothing got done in Bianca's world without detailed lists. Sometimes she even made lists of lists. But her curiosity of when she'd see Leo again was a constant distraction.

CHAPTER NINE

BEING A PRINCE did have its drawbacks.

From marrying out of duty to his lack of anonymity.

Leo might have grown up in the spotlight but that didn't mean he'd grown accustomed to always standing out in a crowd. Instead, he found ways of creating his own privacy. One such way was moving into his own private apartment right here in the palace.

He made his bed every morning. He picked up around the apartment. He liked a neat space. He cooked for himself regularly during the week. He had to admit that cleaning wasn't his thing and so he did let the staff go through the apartment once a week vacuuming, dusting and tidying everything.

But when it came to cooking, he found, to his mother's horror, that he enjoyed it. He had taken many lessons from the palace chef over the years. Not that he was an expert now, but he could make a number of reasonably easy dishes. Tonight's menu included a tossed salad followed by fettuccine Alfredo.

He set the small table on the balcony. It was

simple but cozy. He assured himself that it was nothing more than he would do for a friend. Then again, maybe not just any friend—

Knock. Knock.

He gave the table one last glance and then headed for the door. When he swung it open and found Bianca standing there, he told himself that his racing heart was due to rushing around to get ready for the evening. It had absolutely nothing to do with how beautiful Bianca looked that evening.

She was wearing a black dress that dipped at the neckline, giving a hint of her cleavage. The straps over her shoulders left her arms bare. A belt showed off her delicate waist. The skirt stopped a couple inches above her knees. And on her feet were black sandals.

She was a knockout. He swallowed hard, hoping his voice didn't fail him. "You look amazing."

Suddenly his dark-wash jeans and white oxford shirt seemed quite underwhelming. "I should have told you tonight would be casual. My apologies." He moved to the side. "Come in."

She stepped inside and looked around. "Is this your place?"

"It is."

As she stepped to the center of the living room, she said, "It's like a home within a home."

"It's my private space. It's where I can unwind and be myself."

"It's very nice. And much more modern than the other parts of the palace."

"How is your office? Is it to your liking?"

"Yes, thank you. I like it a lot."

Things between them took on a nervous tension. He wondered if she was remembering their moment in the gardens. If they hadn't been interrupted, things definitely would have escalated. Not wanting to make this evening more awkward, he pushed aside the thoughts.

He cleared his throat. "I apologize for being detained the last couple of days. Something urgent came up and it took all of my time."

"No need to apologize. As a prince, your time must be constantly in high demand. And I was busy getting caught up on wedding details."

He nodded in understanding. He was grateful she'd let him off the hook so easily. Though he was busy catching up on matters of state, as well as busy searching for a wife, he'd needed the time to gather his senses where Bianca was concerned. She was the wedding planner—nothing more.

"And thank you for hiring Sylvie." Bianca's voice interrupted his thoughts. "I think we're going to work well together." Then Bianca frowned. "Will she be joining us this evening? Should I have waited for her?"

"No. This dinner meeting is just for us. I think you have some information to share with me and I have some to share with you."

"It sounds like this is going to be a very productive meal."

"I hope so."

He poured her a glass of white wine. He'd had two cases of each type of wine shipped from the Barto Vineyard. He wondered if she'd notice.

This had to be a dream.

A cozy dinner for two. Just her and a prince. A gorgeous, handsome, dashing prince. Definitely a dream.

And there was music playing in the background. There was the distinct moan of a saxophone floating ever so softly through the dimly lit room. If she were to close her eyes, it'd be so easy to imagine this was a date. A smile lifted her lips.

But this wasn't a date. Far from it. Bianca's eyes opened. This was a business dinner. She couldn't let herself forget it. Just like she'd forgotten what they'd been talking about.

Her gaze met his expectant one. She glanced down, remembering the glass of wine in her hand. Oh, yes, she was supposed to sample the wine.

First, she swirled the wine, inhaling its fruity fragrance. And then she sipped it. Immediately a moan escaped her lips.

Her gaze moved to meet his. "How did you know?"

"Know what?"

"That this is my favorite wine."

"I didn't. But I recalled you drinking it after the wedding at the villa."

"You're a very observant man."

"I try. I hope you're equally as impressed with the dinner."

"It certainly smells good." She reached for her tablet. "Before we eat—"

"No work before dinner. It'll ruin your appetite."

"But we have so much to go over and not much time until the wedding."

"There will be time tonight. I promise. But first, we eat."

He led her to a private balcony. The view of the lush manicured lawn stretched out before her. This place, it was amazing. It was like something written in a storybook. And yet it was real. She wondered what it must have been like to grow up in a place like this.

"This is beautiful. I just love what I've seen of Patazonia."

Leo stepped up next to her. "I get so busy that I rarely stop to appreciate the view."

Was he saying that he didn't regularly have romantic dinners here? The thought of him sharing this kind of moment with another woman soured her mood. Shc gave herself a mental shake. Where had that thought come from? It wasn't like she had a claim on him.

When she went to turn, she realized just how close he was standing. Her heart pounded in her chest. When she inhaled, she breathed in the light scent of his spicy aftershave mingled with his manly scent. It was quite an intoxicating combination.

He didn't move. He stood there right in front of her. All she had to do in that moment was to lift up on her tiptoes. Her gaze dipped to his mouth—his very kissable mouth. And then she could press her lips to his.

The temptation was more than she could take. After all, he was the one to set up this very intimate dinner. Surely, he expected more to happen than business. Right?

With him staring into her eyes, she lifted up on her tiptoes. The common sense in her head was drowned out by the pounding of her heart. His hands reached out to her, wrapping around her waist, drawing her closer.

She leaned forward—

Beep. Beep. Beep.

As though the spell had been lifted, Bianca pulled back.

Beep. Beep. Beep.

Leo inhaled an unsteady breath. "Sorry. It's the kitchen timer."

He turned and headed inside. Bianca paused on the balcony, trying to slow the pounding of her heart. What in the world had gotten into her?

Well, he was amazingly handsome. He was available—sort of. He was, after all, a prince. And she didn't have a drop of royal blood—at least not that she knew of. And then the memory of her mother's journal entry came rushing back to her.

The uncertainty cast over her and her siblings brought her feet back to the ground. What was she going to do if she wasn't a blood Bartolini? Would her siblings look at her differently?

She pushed the troubling thoughts to the back of her mind. There was nothing she could do about her siblings and the fallout from their parents' deaths now. The only thing she could control was giving Giselle the very best wedding and growing her business as a result.

This meal was going to be a challenge. How was she supposed to sit there as the last rays of the sun disappeared and the stars twinkled overhead and stare across the table at the most handsome man and keep her thoughts focused on work?

She walked to the galley kitchen. "Can I help?"

"Would you mind grabbing that basket of bread?"

She turned to the counter and found the bread. "Anything else?"

He shook his head. In his hands were two plates of pasta. "I already put the salad on the table."

She didn't miss how amazing this dinner smelled. Her stomach rumbled its approval. "Did you make all of this?"

He set the food on the table. "Not the bread. I cheated and stole it from the palace kitchen. No one can beat their fresh bread."

He pulled out a chair for her and she sat down. She was tempted to ask if he went to all this trouble for every business meeting but didn't want to ruin this moment. She knew later, when she was alone in her room, that she would replay this evening in vivid detail.

Dinner was quiet without the constant interruption of his phone—or hers for that matter. She knew why hers was quiet—she'd totally muted it. It was a habit she'd gotten into before important meetings. There was nothing worse than a creative and productive meeting halted for a phone call that could wait until another time. In the time it took to answer the call, ideas may have been lost, enthusiasm for a more daring, more bold idea may have waned. And the thing Bianca disliked the most was letting a good idea slip away.

But right now, her ideas had strayed from flower arrangements and quartets to something far more daring—far bolder. As the prince ran the fine linen napkin over his lips one last time, she couldn't help but stare. She wondered what would have happened if they hadn't been interrupted out on the balcony.

In this very intimate setting with no guards, no family—absolutely no one to interrupt them—

would they have even made it to dinner? Or would they be enjoying something far more delicious—

"What is it?" The prince's deep voice rumbled across the table, drawing her from her thoughts.

Did he know what she'd been thinking? No. Impossible. It was best to move things along to the business of the wedding. It would focus her thoughts. And once they wrapped things up, she'd be on her way before her thoughts had another chance to stray again.

She swallowed hard. "Thank you for dinner. It was delicious."

He shook his head. "You don't have to say that."

Was he serious? He doubted his skills in the kitchen? Was it possible a prince could have normal insecurities like everybody else in the world? "You're a talented cook."

Was it possible he was blushing? He moved so quickly to clear the dishes from the table that she wasn't able to get a good look at his face. Perhaps it was a figment of her imagination.

Then realizing she was just sitting there with the prince waiting on her, she jumped to her feet. "Let me help."

"I've got it."

"It's the least I can do after that amazing dinner." She followed him to the kitchen with the near-empty breadbasket.

He placed the plates in the sink and then he turned, almost bumping into her. "I can take that."

He placed the basket on the counter. "Would you like some more wine?"

She shook her head. "No. I mean, I would but I still have work to do."

"Oh, yes. The wedding. Let's go to the living room and you can tell me your thoughts."

Her gaze strayed to the sink. "I should help you wash the dishes."

"There's no need because as much as I like to pretend that this apartment is my space to maintain, there's a staff that periodically puts everything to rights."

"Must be nice."

He smiled and set her heart pounding. "There are some advantages to being the crown prince."

"Talk about a charmed life," she teased.

The smile slipped from his face. "There's a lot more to it than most people know. There are expectations and demands. Sometimes your life is not your own."

"Sorry. I didn't mean anything by the comment."

He shook his head. "It's okay. How about we work on the wedding plans?"

Together they moved to the couch. Leo cleared off the coffee table and Bianca spread out her stuff. She wasn't exactly sure how this was to work. The truth was this evening was feeling more like a date than a business meeting.

A nervous giggle bubbled up in the back of her throat. She choked it down. She had to keep her

composure, even if she was a jittery ball of nerves on the inside. What was it about this man that had her losing her calm, collected demeanor?

CHAPTER TEN

TWO LIT CANDLES.

Two wine glasses.

And this wasn't a date?

Bianca turned a questioning gaze to Leo, finding him sitting closer than she'd anticipated. When his dark, probing gaze met hers, her mouth grew dry. Did he have any idea how his close proximity made her heart pound? What exactly did he have in mind for this evening? Was she going to be dessert?

"Did you have a question for me?" Leo asked.

Act professional. Don't let him see how he gets to me.

She swallowed, hoping her voice didn't betray her. "Um, yes, I'm not sure how this is going to work. Are you planning to have input into the wedding? Or are you just looking for an overview?"

"An overview."

Thank goodness. There were already enough people fighting to have their way with the wedding. "Would you like an overview of everything? Or is there a specific area you're interested in? Such as the disagreements between the queen and the princess?"

His eyes widened with her last question. "I would be most interested in the differing opinions."

Bianca nodded. "Will you make the final decision in those cases?"

A thoughtful look came over his face. "Am I to take it that you would prefer if I were to take on a more active role?"

Bianca resisted the urge to shrug her shoulders. Though the prince had taken on a friendly persona with her, she realized their relationship was still grounded in business. And as a professional, she tried to maintain certain standards that left out shrugging.

She swallowed. "I believe if you were to take on such a role it would help alleviate some of the tension flowing between mother and daughter."

He nodded. "Then I will do it. Anything to bring some peace back to the palace."

"Great." She picked up her tablet. Her finger moved over the screen, searching for the photos she'd taken earlier. "The first disagreement is about the setting for the ceremony."

The prince sighed.

Bianca paused and turned to him. "Have you changed your mind about being the deciding voice?"

"No. Continue."

"Your sister is interested in having a small, intimate ceremony. The queen says she has a long list of relatives and dignitaries that must be allowed to attend without insulting anyone. I can see both points of view."

Frown lines bracketed his eyes. "I really want my sister to have the wedding of her dreams, but I know there are a lot of influential people that will expect an invitation."

"Would you mind if I made a suggestion?"

"Please do."

"What if we were to have the ceremony in the cathedral as your mother wants, but in order to create a cozy intimate ceremony, we can dim the stained-glass windows with curtains and we could use candles to illuminate the aisle and the front of the church. The focus then would be on the happy couple and the wedding party."

Prince Leo paused as though considering all sides of the scenario. And then he looked at her. "I like it. Do it."

"Your mother might not like it—"

"Leave her to me. Make the arrangements. Now, what else is there?"

They went over the guest list, trying to trim it back to the size to fit in the cathedral. The princess and the queen couldn't agree on who should be cut on the list so the formal invitations could be sent out. Surprisingly, Leo was able to glance down over the list and cut the necessary names.

"And how about my sister's dress?"

Bianca struggled to hide a smile. "She has that

under control. No one is to see the dress. It is under lock and key in her suite of rooms. Only her and the dressmaker have access to it."

"My mother must be having a fit."

"I couldn't say. But your sister appears quite pleased with her selection. She said it's a real head turner."

"Oh, no. I'm afraid to imagine."

"Your mother said she won't stand for anything inappropriate so she's having her bridal gown re-sized for the princess."

Leo didn't bother hiding the fact that he rolled his eyes. "Those two are so stubborn. Should I be worried about my sister's selection?"

"I can't honestly say. I haven't seen the dress. But your sister seems reasonable to me."

"That's what I was hoping you'd say."

Now was the time for her to inquire about her compensation for planning the wedding, but how did one ask a prince if he'd followed through with what he'd promised her?

Hey, did you get a chance to call anyone? Um... do you want me to give you ideas—?

"It's my turn." Leo got up and moved to the desk in the next room, which looked to be his study. He returned with a laptop. "As soon as we came to an agreement, I had my people start on preliminary campaigns for your wedding business."

"Wow. You are very efficient." The words were

already out of her mouth by the time she realized she wasn't talking to just anyone. Heat rushed to her cheeks. Leo was a prince, the crown prince. Soon he would be ruling a nation. Of course, he would be on top of things.

"I have five different approaches for you to consider." He acted as though she hadn't just stuck her shimmery heels in her mouth. It made her like him even more.

They went over the different themes. First, flowers everywhere. Second, location shots of her family's estate. Third, following an actual wedding. Fourth, a modern approach with romantic words for art. And last, her as the spokesperson and model.

The proposal was quite involved, more so than she'd ever imagined. "These are all so impressive. Would you mind if I took the night to consider them all?"

"Not at all. Take as long as you need."

"It won't take me long. It's just that the busy day is catching up with me."

"Of course. And I have some phone calls to return before I can call it a night."

She gathered her things. His fingers brushed over hers as he attempted to help her. His touch was like a jolt of static electricity. The sensation raced up her arm and settled in her chest where her heart beat wildly. She'd never experienced anything like it before.

She didn't remember moving to the door, but suddenly she was standing there. When she paused and turned back, Leo was standing right there next to her—closer than two business acquaintances and yet too far away for the perfect ending to an intimate dinner.

He didn't say anything.

She stood perfectly still.

And then his gaze lowered to her mouth. Was he going to kiss her? Her heart tumbled in her chest. This moment was surreal. She, Bianca Bartolini, standing in a palace with a dashingly handsome prince standing before her. Not only had he prepared her dinner but now he might actually kiss her.

If this was a dream, she didn't want to wake up. She was quite content to live the rest of her days in this delicious fantasy.

With her eyes, she willed him to her—like casting a spell over him. She knew it was ridiculous. Of course, it couldn't work—

But then he was there. His lips pressing to hers. Her heart suspended its pounding in utter shock. Could this be happening? Was Prince Leo really kissing her?

But as his lips moved over hers, as his hands wrapped around her waist, as her body was instinctively drawn to his, as her feet felt as though they were floating, she knew that this moment was real. This moment—this kiss—it was something that she would remember for the rest of her life.

His kiss was gentle at first but as she opened herself up to him, he wanted more and so did she. As the blood warmed in her veins, her responses to him became bolder. A deep moan of ecstasy filled the air. Was that her? Or was it him? In that moment, it didn't matter. Each was getting lost in this exquisitely sweet moment—

Knock. Knock.

They jumped apart.

Leo looked at her with desire still smoldering in his eyes. He ran a hand over his disheveled hair. Had she done that? Things had certainly moved beyond a simple good-night kiss.

Her fingers traced over her still-tingling lips. All the while, she couldn't bear to take her eyes off him.

He cleared his throat. "I need to get this."

She nodded in understanding and then stepped back out of the way of the door. Luckily for her, the door would shield her because she had no doubt that one look at her and whoever was on the other side of the door would know what she'd been up to—getting lost in the steamy kisses of the prince.

Leo swung the door open. "Oscar, I thought I'd left strict instructions that I wasn't to be disturbed this evening."

Bianca wondered how far he'd anticipated that

good-night kiss going. Had it been a sudden flare of passion? Or had it been something he'd been planning, anticipating even?

The last thought doused the remaining embers of passion as well as the hope that once the door closed, they would pick up where they'd left off.

"Sir," Oscar said with a baritone voice, "my apologies. It's the princess—"

"Is something wrong with Giselle?"

"No, sir. It's just she's been searching for Miss Bartolini. When she didn't find her in her room, she started searching for her. And when she couldn't find her anywhere, she worried that she'd wandered off sightseeing and perhaps had gotten lost."

Bianca took a couple steps back. She couldn't help but smile at the older man's obvious discomfort of delivering this news to the crown prince. And the frown that covered Leo's face was cute.

"She's not lost," Leo ground out. "She's here. We were just finishing our meeting."

"Very good, sir. I will let the princess know."

"And Oscar?"

"Yes, sir. No more interruptions."

Leo closed the door with a firm thud. Then he turned to her. "I'm sorry about that. Leave it to my sister to jump to farfetched conclusions."

"I should go." Thankfully it was Giselle searching for her, but it could have been the queen. Bianca didn't have to wonder what the queen would think of her lip-locking with the prince. The queen would have her on the first flight out of Patazonia.

"You don't have to." His eyes pleaded with her. "Not yet."

It was so tempting to stay—to find out where that kiss would lead them. But then again, she didn't have to stay to learn the answer to that question. She already knew if she were to stay that they were going to cross over a line they couldn't come back from. And that wasn't something she was ready to do. Not even for a strikingly handsome prince.

And now she had to leave before the little bit of common sense failed her. Because when she stared into his mesmerizing eyes, like she was doing right now, it was so easy to lose herself.

She glanced away. She had to stay focused on her job. It was important. Kissing the prince was not on any of her lists. The lists would get her what she wanted—her successful business, her security. She had to focus on her lists and not on how his enchanting kisses could cast the most delightful spell over her.

"I should be going," she said, glancing down at her hands.

"Are you sure I can't tempt you to stay a little longer? I still have some more of your favorite wine and I have some moonlight I can show you out on the veranda."

Did he have to make this so hard? It was as

though she had a devil on one shoulder, telling her to live in the moment, and an angel on the other, telling her to march out that door. To say she was torn between her desires and her common sense was an understatement.

"As tempting as the offer is, if I don't go to the princess and find out what she needs, I'm pretty certain Oscar will be back. And I feel bad for him—being caught in between you and your sister."

"My sister can't possibly need anything important at this hour. Whatever it is can wait until morning."

"With the wedding so close, it might be urgent."

He rubbed the back of his neck. "Very well. We will meet again tomorrow evening."

Bianca nodded. "As per our agreement."

He opened the door for her. She moved past him, leaving a wide berth between them.

"Good night," she said.

"Till tomorrow."

His words sent a wave of excitement fluttering through her chest. Was that some sort of promise of more delicious kisses to come?

She kept moving down the hallway, not trusting herself to slow down and have one last backward glance. Because she'd been listening for the door to close behind her and it hadn't. Leo was standing there, watching her walk away.

It wasn't until she turned the corner that she

stopped for a moment to gather herself. Had that really happened? She touched a finger to her well-kissed lips. Oh, yes, it had.

The moment though sweet and spicy must be a thing of the past. It was a memory she would hold dear. But now that she could once again think straight, she knew the knock had been her saving grace. Because to have a fling with the prince was to risk her entire future, which had enough uncertainty already. It was best that it ended here.

CHAPTER ELEVEN

HE'D BARELY SLEPT.

And he had no appetite.

In the two weeks since that earth-shifting kiss, Leo had taken every precaution not to be alone with Bianca. What was wrong with him? He'd never had a woman get under his skin the way Bianca had done. When he was around her, he longed to pull her into his embrace.

And that's exactly why they didn't dine alone again. They'd had their business dinners in the village a few nights, another night he'd invited Giselle and William to accompany them. Yet another night they'd had a working dinner with Sylvie. He'd even considered dining with his mother just so they wouldn't be alone, but he wasn't quite that desperate—yet.

Now, he sat alone in his office with two stacks of paper in front of him. They were the bios of candidates for his future wife. He'd been through the pages countless times. With his sister's wedding now only four weeks away, he had to get serious about his search. With a large portion of bios cast into the not-a-chance pile, it was time to meet the remaining women face-to-face.

A frown pulled at his lips. Why had he agreed to this? Oh, yes, so his mother would go along with his plan to let Bianca coordinate his sister's wedding. And now he had to hold up his end of the agreement.

The task left a sour feeling in the pit of his stomach. No wonder he'd skipped breakfast. Who could eat when they had to pick a marriage partner from a stack of biographies of strangers? Well, that wasn't entirely true. Some of the women he'd met on formal occasions. However, he hadn't dated any of them. He knew if he were ever to indicate a liking for someone his mother deemed appropriate, he would be formally engaged by the end of the day.

Maybe that would have been better than sitting here playing Russian roulette with his future. But there was something he'd rather be doing. He'd rather see how the wedding plans were progressing. Judging by the glance he'd had at dinner of Bianca's to-do list, she was hard at work.

He'd never met a person who ran their life by lists. He wouldn't be surprised if Bianca had lists for her lists. He had a lot of things to do as the next King of Patazonia, but even he left room for the unexpected—for a chance to enjoy life. He wondered if Bianca ever let herself enjoy spontaneous moments.

"Sir, your lunch date is here," Oscar said, standing in the open doorway of his office.

He checked the time. She was a half hour early. Normally he appreciated a visitor being prompt, even a few minutes early, but thirty minutes early. That was too much.

"Please tell Miss Ferrara that I'll be with her shortly. I have a few things I must finish up."

"Very well, sir." Oscar nodded and then backed into the hallway and walked away.

He liked Oscar. The older man was very good about keeping his thoughts to himself, unless Leo pushed for an answer. Other than that, the man did what was asked of him without causing any problems. The queen could take a few lessons from him.

"What are you doing in here?" came a familiar voice from the hallway.

He glanced up as his mother strode into his office. She didn't smile, but then again, she rarely smiled so that wasn't unusual. But by the etched lines across her forehead, she did have something on her mind.

"Mother, this is where I work."

"But you have a guest."

He arched a brow. "How would you know?"

She sighed. "Leopold, I thought you'd realized I know everything that goes on within these palace walls. Just like I know you've been spending far too much time with that…that person."

"I believe you mean with the wedding planner. And her name is—"

"I know what her name is. My question is what are you doing having intimate dinners with her?"

Leo refused to let his mother see that her question had poked him the wrong way. He met her gaze straight on. "They aren't intimate." Not anymore. "They are working dinners. Every evening, she dines with me and gives me a status report on the plans for the wedding."

His mother crossed her arms. "You expect me to believe you're really that interested in your sister's wedding? It's just an excuse to spend more time with that woman."

"Bianca is her name. And I'd appreciate you using her name instead of calling her that woman—"

"See, I was right. She's here because you're interested in her."

"She's here because you won't let Giselle have a hand in planning her own wedding and I don't have the patience nor the time to babysit the two of you."

His mother huffed. "Well, your dinner tonight will have to be cancelled."

"And why would that be?"

"Because I've invited the Duke of Lamar and his daughter to dinner. You will be there and you will spend some time with her."

"So this isn't a state dinner, it's a matchmaking ploy."

"Call it what you will, but you can't put off this

marriage much longer. The press is already running negative stories about the royal family and your sister's wedding isn't enough to sway the growing discontent with the citizens. They believe you have no interest in governing this nation. And frankly, I'm starting to think they might be right."

Leo stood. "If you believe that then you don't know me at all."

His mother arched a penciled brow. "Then I will see you at dinner."

He didn't want to go. He wanted to dine with Bianca. He'd been looking forward to that dinner—to, um, hearing about the latest wedding plans.

"I'll be there."

Without a word, his mother turned toward the door. "Don't keep your visitor waiting."

And with that his mother was gone.

His jaw tightened. He hated when his mother started throwing her weight around. He knew he'd started it by hiring Bianca without discussing it with the queen. But he knew she would have vetoed the idea. So he figured it was better to hire Bianca and hope for understanding than to mention it first and then go against his mother's wishes.

When he'd hired Bianca, he'd never imagined she'd be such good company. He wondered what she was doing now. He grabbed his phone to text her.

Are you busy?

He waited. No response.

Can't make dinner. Sorry. Something came up.

With a sigh, he placed his phone in his pocket. He'd put off meeting with—he glanced at his calendar—Jasmine Ferrara long enough. This was going to be more of a business interview than a date because he didn't have any interest in romance.

His thoughts returned to Bianca. He hoped cancelling dinner wouldn't cause any problems. From what he could see so far, Bianca was quite capable of making sensible decisions concerning the wedding. She didn't need him looking over her shoulder, but he wasn't willing to let go of their connection. He needed to be on top of things should his mother decide to cause trouble.

Or at least that's what he told himself was the reason for insisting on dining with Bianca each evening. It had absolutely nothing to do with that unforgettable kiss. After all, he was supposed to be interviewing for a wife. He didn't have the right to kiss Bianca—even if it had been the best kiss ever.

How could the day be over already?

Where had the time gone?

Bianca made her way back to her office within the palace walls. She had so many notes. It was going to take her hours to sort through everything. But she was supremely pleased with how much she'd accomplished.

The ceremony, as well as the extensive security, had been planned down to the finest detail. And though it'd been a heated meeting with the queen and her wedding planner, they'd finally struck an agreement where the queen would get to keep her extensive guest list while the princess got to have a sense of intimacy with lots of candles and curtains that would be lowered over the stained-glass windows just as the ceremony was about to begin.

Bianca smiled as she entered the office.

"There you are." Sylvie glanced up. "I've been trying to reach you."

Bianca pulled out her suspiciously quiet phone. The battery was dead. No wonder she hadn't gotten any responses to her inquiries from that morning.

Nor had she heard from Leo. Not that there was any particular reason she should hear from him, but that hadn't kept her from hoping. Just the thought of him had heat rushing to her face.

"What has you blushing?" Sylvie asked.

Bianca swallowed hard. No one could know about the stolen kiss. Not even Sylvie, who was quickly becoming a good friend. The kiss had been a mistake. A moment of passion.

"I'm just warm," she said, hoping Sylvie would believe her and let the subject drop. "I was doing a lot of rushing around. For some reason, I imagined a palace would always be cold and drafty but that isn't the case here. Perhaps I should have packed more summer clothes."

"There are some great shops in the village. I could write down their names."

She didn't have time for shopping. It wasn't on her list of things to do. And she had something to do every minute of every day. The wedding was so close and there were still so many details to take care of, including the after-party.

Still, Bianca didn't want to be rude. "Sure. If you could jot those down for me that would be great."

Sylvie smiled. "I'll do that."

Bianca glanced at the time on the wall. "It's getting late. I'm surprised to find you still here."

"I didn't want to go home before you got back. You know, in case you had something that needed done ASAP."

Bianca glanced down at the stack of work she'd placed on her desk. "I do have a lot that needs done, but not tonight."

"Are you sure? I don't have any plans."

"I'm sure," Bianca said. "I need a chance to sort through my notes. I'll have a list for you in the morning."

"Okay. As long as you're sure."

"I am." The truth was she was so accustomed to working on her own that it was taking her some time to get used to having an assistant. "Go get some rest and I'll see you in the morning."

Sylvie grabbed her things and headed for the door. She paused and turned back. "I hope you have a nice dinner with the prince."

There was a look in her eyes like she knew what had gone down between Bianca and Leo. Was it possible rumors had started?

"I don't know what you've heard?"

"Heard?" A look of confusion came over Sylvie's face. "I haven't heard anything. Oh, gosh. I'm sorry. I didn't mean to imply anything. I just—I meant that I hoped everything goes well."

"Oh. Yes. Me too." She felt so ridiculous for thinking her secret had gotten out. She was going to have to be calmer going forward. "I think the prince will be impressed with what I was able to negotiate between the princess and her mother."

"I know that I am. I'm really enjoying working with you. I will see you in the morning. Good night."

"Good night."

Sylvie closed the door behind her. Bianca moved to sit down at her desk. She'd put an extra charger cord in her desk. She'd been meaning to replace her battery as it didn't last nearly as long as it once had. But one thing after another kept her from going into the village to buy one. She supposed she could order it online and have it delivered to the palace. Yes, that sounded like the best idea.

She plugged in her phone but it was so dead that it didn't immediately turn on. She set it aside to do its thing. But she didn't want to be late for dinner. Leo did have a thing for punctuality.

They hadn't discussed what time dinner would be tonight. If it was to be at the same time as usual she had to get moving. She didn't even have time to stop at her room and change clothes.

Bianca checked her makeup with her compact. She powdered her nose before reapplying her shimmery lip gloss. One final glance in the mirror and she decided it would have to do. It wasn't like she was going on a date. Right?

She stood up and checked her phone. It still had that blasted flashing red checkmark on the screen that let her know it was charging, but it wasn't ready to be used, just yet. And so she left it behind.

Thankfully she was good with directions because the palace was full of small staircases tucked discreetly in walls at the most unexpected places. When she reached the knight wearing the palace's coat of arms, she turned and headed up the carpeted steps. They were modest and absolutely nothing like the grand staircase in the front of the palace. If you didn't know about the steps, you might very well miss them.

At the top of the steps, she turned to the left. The prince's apartment was at the end of the hallway. It was very private. In fact, as she glanced around, she realized it was the only doorway. And considering Bianca hadn't passed anyone on her way here, she assumed not many people were welcome in this part of the palace. The fact that she'd been invited into this part of the prince's world made her feel special. A smile pulled at her lips.

She paused outside the apartment door. It was the first time she'd allowed herself to imagine how this evening might go. She envisioned another candlelight dinner with the prince flirting with her. Would it be proper to flirt back? Oh, who cared about proper? This was a fantasy.

Part of her said that she needed to stay focused on business, but the womanly part of her said that she was crazy to pass up a moment in Leo's arms. After all, what were the chances that another handsome prince would cross her path?

She halted her thoughts. She couldn't believe she was having this debate. It wasn't like the kiss would happen again. It was a fluke. A one-time thing.

With the internal conflict resolved, she leveled her shoulders and lifted her chin. It was time to do business. She inhaled a deep breath, hoping to slow her heartbeat. She raised her hand and knocked.

No response.

Perhaps she hadn't knocked loud enough. She tried again.

Still nothing.

She turned and retraced her steps. At the bottom of the steps, she came across Oscar.

"Good evening, ma'am."

"Hi. Would you happen to know where the prince might be?"

"I just passed him heading into the gardens. But he—"

"Thank you. I'm late." She rushed off.

The gardens were down another floor. But when she got to the window, she saw Leo was already outside. Had he planned on having dinner in the gardens? The thought of such a beautiful romantic setting set her heart aflutter.

She started moving again, anxious to catch up with him. But when she reached the main floor and made her way out to the patio area, Leo was nowhere in sight. She set off down one of the paths but the shrubs and trees acted as walls, making the gardens more like a maze.

And then she spotted Leo just up ahead. She was about to call out to him when she noticed he wasn't alone. Bianca moved forward just enough to catch sight of a young woman smiling up at him. From that distance, Bianca couldn't make out what he was saying but whatever it was had his female companion thoroughly enthralled.

But then again, with his deep, rich voice he

could be reading the information on the back of a medicine bottle and make it sound engaging. An uneasy feeling settled in the pit of her stomach.

Bianca took a step back. She didn't want them to see her lurking. Her foot landed on a fallen twig. The sound of cracking wood was much louder than she would have expected. Knowing it would draw attention, she jumped behind a bush. Her white heels sunk in the freshly watered dirt.

Tears stung the backs of her eyes. She told herself it was her being upset over ruining her cloth pumps and not the fact that Leo had gone from kissing her like she was the only woman in the world to romancing some other woman in the gardens instead of having dinner with her.

The murmur of voices faded away. They must have moved on. It was then that Bianca glanced around the bush, praying no one was around to witness her most embarrassing moment. To her relief, she was alone.

She stepped back upon the stone walkway. In the waning sunlight, she glanced down at her shoes. They were ruined—along with her daydream that the prince thought she was special. She was just another woman in his long list of admirers.

Avoiding the palace staff, she made her way back to her office where she retrieved her phone and a stack of work. She headed to her bedroom, skipping dinner altogether. She had no appetite.

Once in her room with the door closed, she looked at her phone. Now, it was charged and there were a couple of text messages. The first was from Sylvie. The second was from Leo, cancelling their dinner plans. And that was it. No explanation. No nothing.

She wanted to be angry with him, but she knew that wasn't logical. It wasn't like they were seeing each other. The kiss had been a mistake. They had a business relationship. Nothing more.

She would do well to remember that.

She needed to focus on her work. It was the only thing she could count on—the only thing in her life that she felt as though she had any control over.

CHAPTER TWELVE

SHE WAS TIRED of the games.

The prince could not kiss her one evening and then share moonlight walks with someone else another night. It didn't work that way. It didn't matter that he was a prince or that her heart raced every time they were in the same room. She had her standards.

And that's why for the next ten days, she'd reduced their meetings to daily status emails. It was much more efficient. And so much safer for her heart.

However, when she glanced up from her desk to find Leo standing in the doorway of her office, she was caught off guard.

She swallowed hard. "Your Highness, I wasn't expecting you. Can I do something for you?"

"Your Highness?" He frowned at her. "We're back to using titles?"

She gave a slight shrug before saving the current document on her laptop. She had a feeling the prince's visit would take a bit of time.

"Today is the final day of the queen's *la fête*."

"La fête?"

"Yes. Technically it's my mother's sixtieth

birthday but she refuses to celebrate her birthday. She says she's too old to have birthdays. So they call her celebration the queen's *la fête*."

"Oh, I see. I'll make sure to keep out of the way. Besides I have plenty of work to do—"

"No, you don't understand. You are invited."

Bianca pressed a hand to her chest. "Me. But I'm a nobody."

"You are my guest."

Her heart stuttered. Was he asking her to be his date? Wait. No. He must mean his guest as in a general invitation because he'd moved on to that woman in the gardens. Bianca's mood dampened a bit.

She shook her head. "I couldn't intrude. It should be a private family event."

"It's not private nor a family-only event. This will be a big state dinner with fireworks afterward."

"Fireworks?" Now that was her kind of party.

He smiled and nodded. "And there is a place at the table with your name on it."

"But what's the dress code?"

"Formal."

"As in black tie?"

He nodded. "If that is a problem—"

"I've got a formal gown, but I had planned to wear it to your sister's wedding."

"Then I will see that you get a new gown for the wedding."

"No, you can't. That would be too much."

"You are doing me the favor. It is the least I can do."

"How so?"

"Because these events are usually stuffy and can veer into matters of state. I would like to avoid that this evening. And with you there, it will make the evening more festive. Perhaps the politics can be avoided for one evening. Your attendance would be in honor of the queen."

When he put it that way, how could she say no?

"Okay. I'll go."

"Good. I can stop by your room on the way to the cocktail hour."

That would be too much like a date and she needed to make sure the boundaries were clear. She couldn't let herself get swept up in the evening. She was hired help. Nothing more.

"It's okay. I'll make my way."

His eyes reflected disappointment, but in a blink it was gone. "Very well. Cocktails are at six in the library."

"I'll see you there." Bianca turned back to her laptop. She had so much work to do.

But she couldn't stop thinking about the fact that the prince had given her a personal invitation to a very important dinner. The thought of spending the evening with Leo made her heart race.

She told herself not to get too excited about it because they would be surrounded by heads of state and dignitaries. And then there was the queen. Bianca didn't care how much she told herself otherwise, that woman made her nervous.

This was it.

This was as good as it got.

Bianca gave her coral gown with its ivory and silver embellishments one last glance in the mirror. Her stomach shivered with nerves. She had no idea if she was overdressed or underdressed. Perhaps she should have consulted Giselle. She most likely wouldn't have minded giving her some fashion tips. But it was too late for that now.

She ran a hand over her pulled-up hair. It was then that she noticed the slight tremor in her hands. How could she have gone to some of the biggest weddings in the world with Hollywood stars and politicians but this birthday party made her quake.

Bianca sucked in a deep breath. She had to get a grip. She checked the time on the delicate diamond-studded watch that her parents had given her on her sixteenth birthday. It was stunning and something she wore only on the most special of occasions. But when she wore it, no matter where she was in the world, it made her feel like her family was a little closer. And now with her parents both gone, that connection was more important to her than ever before.

Sometimes she felt like a leaf just tumbling in

the wind. There was no true place where she fit in. Her brother knew it. Her sister wouldn't say it, but she couldn't deny it.

But if Bianca were to make her wedding business a success, she would have a sense of security. She couldn't control the outcome of the DNA tests, but she could control the success of this wedding—so long as she stayed on top of every detail.

Buzz. Buzz. Buzz.

Her cell phone vibrated against the white marble vanity. Knowing it could be about any number of things regarding the quickly approaching wedding, she rushed to grab it. When the caller ID showed her sister's name, worry consumed Bianca for an entirely different reason.

"Gia, are the test results in?"

"Well, hello to you too." Gia expelled an exasperated breath.

"Sorry. It's just all this waiting. It's getting to me." If anyone would understand, it was her sister.

"You don't have to worry."

"What's that supposed to mean?"

"It's obvious you're a Bartolini. You look just like Nonna when she was your age."

"You really think so?" Bianca once more glanced in the mirror. She didn't see it.

"I do. I'm the one who should be worried."

"No, you shouldn't. You were Papa's favorite. And you can't deny it."

There was a moment of silence before Gia said, "That leaves Enzo."

They both hurriedly agreed that it couldn't be him. Could it? Secretly Bianca wondered if it was him as he and their father used to butt heads—a lot.

She stifled a sigh. The guessing game was getting old. And it was getting them no closer to the answers they so desperately needed.

They talked for a few more minutes, catching up on each other's lives. Then Bianca had to go. She couldn't be late for the queen's celebration. She promised to speak to Gia soon.

Bianca headed out the door. Truth be told, she wasn't sure where she was going, but she'd been too proud to admit that to Leo. But she figured if she could make it to the main entrance that she could just fall in line with the other guests as they made their way to the library.

And that's exactly what she did. Security was everywhere in dark suits and wearing earpieces. Since she was a guest within the palace, she was able to pass through the checkpoint without any problems.

She wondered if security was always this heavy. And then she realized that it would be this intense for the wedding. She would have to make allowances for that in her plans. She reached for her phone to make a note and then realized she'd left it back in her room. She tucked the information in the back of her mind.

She followed two couples to the library. As she glanced around, she was relieved to find her dress would fit in. At last, she took a full breath.

She could do this.

The funny thing was that everyone thought she didn't get nervous or filled with anxiety before a big event she'd planned. That wasn't true, but she didn't tell them. The trick was to put on a confident smile and never let them see her perspire. And that's what she intended to do this evening.

As she stepped into the massive room, she immediately searched for Leo. He was tall, so she hoped he would stand out in this crowd, but she didn't see him. And before she had a chance to make the rounds, Giselle rushed up to her.

"There you are." Giselle slipped her arm in Bianca's. "I've been telling everyone how you are putting a fresh spin on the wedding."

Was that what she was doing? Who was she to argue with a client? Correction: a princess.

"Bianca, I'd like to introduce you to the Duchess of Lamar."

Not sure how to properly greet a duchess, she said, "It's a pleasure to meet you."

The wedding conversation took off from there. The duchess said that she would be recommending Bianca's services to her nieces. That made Bianca smile.

When they entered the grand dining hall, it was stunning. The table was unlike any she'd ever seen as it must have seated at least a hundred people. Wow! She couldn't even wrap her mind around the size of the long narrow room with purple trim and portraits of the royal family through the generations.

She was seated in the middle of the table. Nowhere close to the queen at the head of the table, which was fine with Bianca. And nowhere close to the prince at the foot of the table, which she found deeply disappointed her.

But she was delighted that throughout the eight-course meal, she was entertained by the Earl of Saskan. By the looks of him, he was only a few years her senior. He was a delightful man, who could easily carry on an entertaining conversation. And he wasn't too bad looking, but he had nothing on the prince.

"It's nice that they invited you to dinner," the earl said. "They have such a tight knit group of people for these events that it's rare for an outsider to be included. Not that you're an outsider, but you know, not one of the group—"

With each word he spoke, her insecurities came rushing to the surface. She was an outsider in this grand, historic palace. Nothing would change that. She even felt out of place in her own family, she thought sadly.

"It's okay." She placed her hand on his forearm

to get his attention. When his rambling stopped, she said, "I understand. I'm a guest at the palace, I believe they felt it would be rude not to invite me."

She felt someone staring at her. Could it be the prince? And then realizing that it was probably inappropriate to be touching the earl, she quickly withdrew her hand. When she lifted her gaze, the prince turned his head to the person on his right. Why should he care who she spoke to?

The earl looked at her with relief written all over his flushed face. "Sometimes, well, a lot of times I say the wrong thing. I didn't mean anything by it."

"No offense taken." But it was definitely time to change the subject. "And how are you connected to the royal family?"

She didn't know it was such a loaded question but it kept the earl talking of his lineage through most of the meal. All she had to do was interject an acknowledgment in the appropriate pauses as he regaled her with a detailed history lesson.

Surprisingly, the dinner didn't last as long as she'd imagined with that many courses. The queen didn't chat abundantly and when she finished the course, she signaled for the dishes to be cleared. In fact, during the salad course, the earl had talked so much that he'd squeezed in only one bite before the dishes were whisked away.

When the meal was over, they were escorted to the grand ball room. And grand it was with its gold trim and enormous landscape murals on the walls. A crystal chandelier was the focal point of the room. Bianca had never seen a chandelier of that magnitude. It took in the light, making the thousands of crystals shimmer and then cast a rainbow of colors throughout the room.

As the music started, Giselle sought her out. "Are you having a good time?"

"I am. Thank you. But I had no idea there would be dancing."

"My mother, though she hasn't danced since my father passed on, does enjoy the music. You should dance."

Bianca shook her head. "I don't think so."

Giselle frowned. "Why not?"

"I really should go back to my room. I have so much work to do—"

"Not tonight. There will be no work. I insist you enjoy yourself." Just then the earl passed by them and Giselle stopped him. "Donatello, my guest doesn't have an escort, would you mind dancing with her?"

The earl's face lit up. He turned to Bianca. "May I have this dance?"

"I… I don't think it's a good idea." She was a wedding planner, not any part of the royal society. It was more than enough that she'd sat at the dining table, but now to kick up her heels—it didn't seem right.

"Go ahead," Giselle encouraged.

The earl turned to Bianca. "If you don't know how to dance, I can show you. Trust me, it's not that hard."

Heat rushed to Bianca's face. How was she supposed to turn him down now? He was such a nice man, but he didn't make her heart race or fill her with giddiness like…like Leo.

In that moment, she realized she had a crush on the prince. Maybe it shouldn't come as such a shock. Probably most of the single women and maybe even some of the married ladies in the room had a crush on him. What wasn't to like?

But she couldn't just stand around here waiting for Leo to ask her to dance. That wasn't going to happen. And the best way to forget about how Leo made her feel was to get on with her life. Just one dance and then she would quietly slip away to her room.

"I'd love to dance." Bianca slipped her hand in the crook of Donatello's arm.

As he led her to the full dance floor, her gaze strayed across Leo's. This time she didn't have to wonder if he was looking at her. He was staring right at her. There was a frown pulling at his kissable lips. And his normally warm brown eyes were dark and stormy.

As the earl took her into his arms, she had to turn away from Leo. What was he frowning about? Leo might have invited her to the dinner, but it wasn't like he was her date. In fact, he hadn't spoken so much as a single word to her all evening. He didn't earn the right to be upset with her. She hadn't done anything wrong.

The earl hadn't been exaggerating about his skill on the dance floor. She knew how to dance, but her moves weren't as smooth as his. As they moved around the floor, she searched for Leo, but she wasn't able to locate him.

Maybe he'd been upset about something else. Yes, that must be it. Someone must have said something he didn't like. Perhaps it was the queen that had him out of sorts. Because there was no way he cared who she danced with.

When the music stopped, Bianca said, "Thank you so much for the dance. I enjoyed it." It was the truth. "And you are quite a talented dancer."

"Thank you. We could go again, if you want."

"Thanks. But I think I'll sit this one out."

"Perhaps later."

She nodded. "Maybe."

And that was it. The earl moved on. Without anyone around that she knew, Bianca was left to her own devices. She made her way to the edge of the crowd. It was time to make a quick exit, but she was on the opposite side of the room from the door.

She stayed near the wall as she made her way around the crowded room. She neared the corner where there were floor-to-ceiling purple drapes with gold trim that framed the wall of windows overlooking the gardens. She paused for just a moment to admire the view.

When she turned to continued walking, someone reached out. A hand pushed against her mouth, muffling her scream. Another arm wrapped around her waist and she was yanked back into the curtains. It all happened so suddenly that she didn't have time to fight back.

CHAPTER THIRTEEN

THE DOOR SLIPPED CLOSED.

Darkness surrounded her.

Bianca's heart raced. She was alone in the pitch black with her kidnapper. Her palms grew moist. Her mouth was dry. She had to do something. Fast.

Having gained her wits, she used all her might and kicked the person behind her. There was the muttering of a male voice. Immediately he released her. She spun around, but she couldn't so much as see her hand in front of her face.

"What'd you go and do that for?"

She immediately recognized that voice. It was Leo. Leo? What was he doing grabbing her out of the ballroom into—whatever this room was?

"Leo? Is that you?"

"Who else did you think it'd be?" He sounded a bit exasperated.

"I don't know. Some kidnapper. Or worse."

"You are safe. It's just me."

Her gaze moved around the room. Even though her eyesight had adjusted to the darkness, she couldn't make out anything, including him. "Leo, what are you doing? Why did you kidnap me from the ballroom?"

"I didn't kidnap you."

"Really? Because it sure seemed like it to me." She turned around. Her hands stretched out in the darkness, searching for the door. "How do I get out of here?"

"Come with me."

"No. Now turn on the lights."

It took a couple of seconds but then a bare lightbulb lit up. She glanced around, finding that they were in some sort of passageway. And she couldn't make out a door.

"Where's the door?"

He pointed to a spot on the wall. It looked like the rest of the wall. And there was no door handle. She moved to it and tried to push it open but it wouldn't budge.

"Bianca, stop." The agitation had drained from his voice. "Let me explain."

Having no success with opening the door, she whirled around to him. "Is there another way out of here?"

"Yes."

"Then let's go."

"Aren't you even going to let me explain?"

She was mad at him. She didn't think anything he had to say at the moment was going to change that fact. "No. Let's go."

He let out a frustrated sigh. "Follow me."

He led her through a tunnel. In places the tunnel narrowed and they had to pass through it sideways. In other places there were wooden stairs.

"What is all of this?" she asked.

"So you're speaking to me again?"

She huffed. If he thought that he was off the hook, he was wrong. She didn't bother answering him. He could come to his own conclusion.

Not pushing his luck, the prince said, "These are secret passages that weave their way through the palace."

"I've heard of palaces having secret passageways but I thought they were just works of fiction."

"Now you know differently."

"But how do you know where you're going? There are so many different ways to go." She stayed close to him so as not to get left behind.

"I learned these tunnels when I was a kid."

"How did you keep from getting lost?"

"I did get lost, but my father found me. He taught me how to navigate the tunnels so I never got lost again. Once you figure it out, it's no harder than walking through the halls of the palace."

"Uh-huh." She didn't believe him.

If she was in here alone, not only would she be scared, but she was certain she'd never find her way out. She'd become a ghost that haunted the palace.

And then a thought came to her. "Is this place haunted?"

"Haunted?"

"Uh-huh. You know, ghosts that got trapped in these passageways."

Leo stopped and turned to her. In the cramped space they ended up being much closer than she was prepared for. His gaze met hers, making her heart pound. That's all it took—a look—for her body to respond to him.

She was so tempted to lift up on her tiptoes and press her lips to his. She wondered how he would react. Would he pull her closer? Would he wrap his arms around her, crushing her soft curves to his very muscular chest?

But that wasn't part of her plan. She was supposed to ignore these unwanted feelings. After all, he had practically kidnapped her from the party. Still, it'd be so easy to just live in the moment—this very intimate and most unique set of circumstances.

As though Leo could sense her conflicted emotions, he leaned forward as though to tip the scales in his favor. The breath hitched in her throat. He was going to kiss her.

But she couldn't let him off the hook that easy. Her hands moved, pressing against his very firm chest. Surprise flashed in his eyes.

"Don't even think about it." As the stern warning passed over her lips, her heart sank in her chest.

"Are you saying the thought hadn't crossed your mind?"

She wasn't playing this game with him because she knew that she would end up losing. "I'm saying that you aren't getting off the hook that easily. Shouldn't you be here with your girlfriend?"

His brows drew together. "What girlfriend? I have no girlfriend."

She desperately wanted to believe him, but she knew what she saw. "The woman you were walking with in the gardens the night you cancelled our dinner plans."

His eyes momentarily widened. "You saw us?"

"I did."

"And that's why you've been so distant?"

"I've been busy." She answered a little too quickly—a little too vehemently.

He nodded in understanding, though they both knew it was much more than work that kept Bianca away from him.

"The woman you saw me with is an old friend of the family. I'm not now nor was I ever interested in her for anything other than friendship. We went for a walk while her father and the queen talked business. That is all."

"Really?" She wanted to take back the question, but it was too late.

"Really."

He said all the right words, but this thing between them—it was like playing with fire. It'd be so easy to get caught up in the flames—and get burned.

And then realizing that she was still touching him—still absorbing his body heat through his white dress shirt—she yanked her hands back to her sides. But it was too late. His energy had been absorbed into her body and it coursed through her faster than the speed of light. It warmed her chest and melted her core into a puddle of need.

No. This isn't going to happen. He isn't going to take what he wants.

She thought of stepping back, allowing more space between them, but she didn't want him to read weakness in her movement. And so she stood there, rooted to the spot. Her determined gaze continued to hold his. She would not let him detect any weakness in her.

But she was starting to wonder how long she could keep this up. Because every fiber of her being craved him.

He stood there for a moment as though questioning her decision. But her determination was stronger than the way his dark eyes could make her knees turn to gelatin. Wasn't it?

Before she could answer that question, he turned and continued through the passageway. She followed him as they ascended a set of narrow steps with no handrail. Bianca pressed her hands to the cold stone walls to balance herself. They kept going up and up. Then there was a switch-back and they ascended another flight of steps.

"Where are we going?"

"We're almost there."

That didn't really answer her question. But she would be grateful to get out of this secret passageway. She felt totally disoriented and utterly reliant on Leo—the man of mystery. She wondered what other secrets he had and if any of them were nearly as interesting as these passageways.

At last they reached a doorway, if it could be called that. It was more like a movable part of the wall. A faint bit of light lit the way.

As they stepped out of the wall, Bianca asked, "Where are we?"

There wasn't a voice to be heard. So they were a long way from the ballroom. And there weren't any other sounds. They were alone. All alone.

Stay focused.

But he's so cute. And what happens here would be our secret.

But he hasn't apologized. He can't just do what he wants without consequences.

Leo turned to her on what appeared to be some sort of landing. There was a set of stairs to his left and a single step that led to a wooden door on his right. The window let in the moonlight.

"We are in the east tower," he said.

Her heart pitter-pattered in her chest.

Why had he brought her here?

* * *

Now that he had her alone, he wasn't sure this was such a good idea. But it was too late to back out now.

"I wanted you to have the best vantage point. Come on." Leo took Bianca's hand and led her up the step and out the door.

"Vantage point for what?" She glanced around.

In the moonlight, the general layout was visible. Leo let go of her hand and lit some torches. A warm glow filled the space and highlighted the large daybed with a twin mattress and a dozen plush pillows.

"What is this place?" Bianca asked.

"It's my private spot. It's where I come when I have a lot on my mind. Sometimes I sleep out here."

He gazed into her eyes.

His heart pounded against his ribs. All he wanted to do was pull her into his arms and crush his lips against hers. He wanted to forget his duty—his obligations. In Bianca's arms, he was certain he would find the release he was seeking.

But when she gazed up at him like he hung the stars—like she was doing now—guilt assailed him.

He needed to be honest with her. She needed to know the real him. Because he wasn't the perfect prince that his mother portrayed to the world.

His thoughts drifted back to the week he'd spent

on this very terrace, refusing to go back inside the palace. It had been the darkest point in his life—

"Leo, what's the matter?" Bianca's voice drew him from his troubled thoughts.

He shook his head. "Nothing."

"It's something. The pain is written all over your face. I'm a pretty good listener—that is if you want to talk about it."

He hadn't talked about it with anyone. Not even his mother. And she had been there—she'd gone through the nightmare, not exactly with him. They'd each gone through it in their own individual ways.

Leo turned and gazed into Bianca's eyes. "I don't want to ruin this night for you."

"You won't. I'd like to think we're friends and that we can confide in each other." She stared into his eyes as though she could see clear through to his soul. "Does it have something to do with your father?"

How did she do that? How did she know what he was thinking? Did she have some sort of special power? Or were his thoughts that transparent?

"How did you know?"

She shrugged. "It was just a guess. But you never talk about him. How come?"

Leo took her hand and led her over to the daybed. They perched on the edge of it. He was trying to find a place to start. He supposed the best place to start was the beginning.

"I'd looked up to my father all of my life. When I grew up, I wanted to be just like him. The problem was that I had no idea what that would entail."

"I can't even begin to imagine. And I thought I had it hard fitting into my family."

He shook his head. "Don't feel sorry for me. I'm not the good guy you think I am."

"Sure you are. Look at what you're doing for your sister. And how you took time out of your busy schedule to attend your friend's wedding. And then there's what you're doing for me—"

"Stop." He held up a hand as though blocking her compliments. "You don't understand. None of that can undo the past."

He recalled how his mother made him promise to never speak of his father's death. She wanted to sweep all the unsavory details under the rug, where no one would notice them. His mother wanted the picture-perfect family and the unblemished prince to ascend to the throne. She wanted to live a lie because none of those things existed in real life.

But he'd already lashed out at his father and it had cost his father his life. Leo couldn't lose his only remaining parent and so he did as the queen wanted. However, it came with a price. Every time he had to gloss over the details or leave out a fact, especially when talking to his own sister, it'd killed a little piece of him.

He'd been living with the secret for so long that

it felt as though it was going to smother him unless he let it out. And Bianca was so easy to talk to. It was though he could tell her anything and she would understand. But would she look at him the same way once he told her his secret?

He drew in an unsteady breath. Peeling back the scabs hurt just like the nightmare had happened yesterday. But this wasn't about his comfort. It was about proving to Bianca that he wasn't worthy of her.

He stared straight ahead into the black sky. "I was sixteen. And I wanted to go on holiday with one of my friends to the lake. But my father told me I had responsibilities to attend to. I was a kid. I hated being in the spotlight. I hated being escorted by bodyguards everywhere. I hated being different."

"It must have been difficult. I think every kid just wants to fit in. I know I did."

Her words of comfort gave him the encouragement he needed to continue. "When I told him I was going with my friends and nothing he said could stop me, my father grew angry and started yelling at me. He told me it was time I grew up. He had plans for me to attend a royal wedding in another country. He said I would meet an appropriate young woman."

Leo could still recall his outrage when he realized his father had already chosen the young woman he was to marry. He wasn't even an adult yet and his whole life had been planned without even consulting him.

"I told him I didn't want to date anyone. My father said this wasn't going to be a date. This young woman would be my future wife." The exact words of that horrific fight were a little lost on him. "My father suddenly grew quiet. I thought it meant he was giving in to my demands. Being a kid, I told him I quit being a prince. That my sister could be queen. By then he was perspiring and his face was a pasty color." Leo could still see his father's sickly image in his mind. "He strode up to me. I never saw him so angry. Ever." Leo's voice faltered. "He told me I couldn't quit. I was a prince by blood. It was an honor—a privilege. And..."

Bianca reached out and squeeze his hand. There was so much to that innocent touch. There was kindness, compassion. Both of which he didn't deserve.

He swallowed hard, hoping his voice wouldn't fail him. He had to get out this secret that he'd been keeping so deep within him. It was as though it was choking him. And the only way he could take a full breath was to get it all out in the open.

"I should have known that something was seriously wrong with him. He'd been sweating profusely and he'd looked awful, but I was only worried about myself and being with my friends. I wasn't giving up. I kept yelling at my father. I..."

I can't believe those angry, hurtful words were the last ones I said to him." Tears stung his eyes as emotion choked off his next words.

Bianca shifted closer to him as though letting him know that she was there to lean on. Then ever so softly, she said, "He knew you loved him."

"Did he? Because when he stopped yelling mid-sentence the look in his eyes was full of rage. And…and then he collapsed." He ran the back of his hand over his eyes. "I don't know how long I stood there like a complete and utter fool."

"You were in shock."

"But it was my father—the king. If I'd acted faster, maybe things would have been different."

"I don't think a few seconds would have changed things. It was out of your hands."

"You might be the only one who thinks that. Because when I finally came to my senses and started screaming for help, my mother entered the room. When she rushed over to my father, she asked me what had happened. I told her we'd been fighting and he'd collapsed. She looked at me as though it was all my fault. Then she made me promise not to mention a word of what had happened to anyone, including my sister."

"That's a huge secret for a kid to keep. Is that why there's a distance between you and your mother?"

He shrugged. "Everything was different after that. She had to become the regent and it was a position she didn't want, but she said that duty must be upheld. So I guess she holds that against me too."

Bianca placed a finger on the side of his jaw, encouraging him to meet her gaze. "And you've been blaming yourself all of this time?"

"It was my fault. If I hadn't been so insistent on having my way, things would have been different."

"Or they might have happened the same way. I don't think anything you said or did would have changed your father having a heart attack. And did you ever think your mother was trying to protect you? Maybe she struggled stepping into such an important role and by taking a firm line, it was her way of proving to everyone, including herself, that she was up to the challenge."

He paused, giving Bianca's words some serious thought. "I never thought of it that way. My mother always seemed so calm, so in control."

"Maybe you only saw what she wanted you to see."

His gaze searched Bianca's. "You really don't think I had any part in my father's death?"

"I don't. And I think if he was here, he'd tell you the same thing."

Those are the words that he'd longed to hear. He just hadn't known it. And having shared his deepest-held secret with Bianca, they now had a bond he knew would never be broken.

* * *

Her heart raced.

She'd never felt as close to anyone as she did in that moment—

A great big boom shook the ground.

Bianca instinctively reached out for Leo. Her fingers wrapped around his muscular bicep.

"Relax," he said. "Everything is okay."

Was it? Okay, that is. Because she was beginning to wonder if those passageways had taken them back in time and they were suddenly a couple hundred years in the past. The boom could be that of a canon aimed at the palace. When she was with Leo, it was easy to believe that anything was possible.

But then again, maybe she'd had one too many sips of champagne. As another softer boom filled the air, she braced herself for the palace to shake, but instead she saw the sky fill with light—colorful shades of pink and blue.

Fireworks. She breathed more easily. And then quickly withdrew her hand from Leo's arm. She moved to the stone wall at the edge of the tower. There wasn't a soul near them. They were so high up that it felt as though they were in the sky with millions of stars sparkling around them.

And then she felt Leo's presence just behind her. She waited for him to reach out and touch her. Her traitorous heart picked up its pace in anticipation.

When she turned her face to him, he said, "I'm sorry. I handled this night all wrong."

He looked at her like she should say something here, but if he was waiting for her to disagree with him, he'd be waiting a long time.

As the silence stretched between them, Leo cleared his throat. "It's just when I saw Donatello flirting with you and you enjoying it…it bothered me."

When his gaze lifted to meet hers, she searched his brown depths. Not finding the answer she was looking for, she asked, "Why did it bother you who I was talking to?"

He stepped closer to her, so close that they were practically touching. All the while the booms of the fireworks sounded in the background and the sky lit up with a rainbow of colors.

And then he reached out to her, caressing her cheek ever so gently. "Because every time you smiled, I wanted you to be smiling at me. And when you let out that contagious bubbly laugh of yours, I wanted it to be because I made you happy. And when you danced, I wanted it to be my arms wrapped around you, holding you close."

She lifted her chin ever so slightly. And then in a breathy voice, she asked, "You did?"

He gave a slight nod of his head. "I did. Do you know how hard I've been fighting my attraction to you?"

"I have some idea. I've been doing the same thing."

Desire reflected in his eyes. "I've wanted to do this since the first moment I spotted you this evening." He lowered his head and caught her lips with his own.

The breath stilled in her lungs. There were a million reasons why this shouldn't be happening. And in that moment, those reasons dissipated into the starry night.

With the cascade of white-and-blue fireworks overhead, Leo's mouth pressed to hers. Her heart leaped into her throat. This was really happening. Leo was kissing her again.

In that moment, it didn't matter that he was a prince. To her, he was just Leo—the man who made her heart race with just a look. There was so much more to him than a fancy title. And she was anxious to continue peeling back the layers that made Leo such an exceptional man.

As his lips moved over hers, she let herself get wrapped up in the moment. The boom and crackle of the fireworks faded into the background. Right now, Leo was shooting off fireworks in her mind…and her heart.

Her arms, almost of their own volition, moved up his chest, over his broad shoulders and wrapped around his neck, drawing him closer. She wanted more. She needed more.

And yet, he took an agonizingly long time savoring her lips—refusing to rush the moment like she was apt to do.

She couldn't tell if it was the boom of the fireworks or the pounding of her heart that filled her ears. Not that it mattered. The only thing she cared about at the moment was that this kiss never ended. Because she knew deep in her heart that this moment was very precious. They were making a memory that she would cherish for the rest of her life.

When Leo pulled back all Bianca wanted to do was to draw him near once more—to feel his warm lips pressed to hers. She struggled to calm her rushed breaths.

"Bianca, if you want me to stop," his voice was raspy as he drew in one quick breath after the other, "tell me now."

Was he serious? "Don't stop."

"You're sure? Because I don't just want you for this moment—I want you to stay the night with me beneath the stars."

She glanced around. "Won't someone find us here?"

A deep laugh bubbled up from deep in his chest. "Trust me, they know better. When I'm up here, I want to be alone."

"And how many other women have you brought here?" She didn't know why she'd asked, but she knew the answer was important to her. The breath hitched in her throat as she waited.

"You, *ma chère*, are the first."

Knowing this was as special to him as it was to her warmed a spot in her chest. She took him by the hand and led him to the daybed. She sank down on the soft cushion as Leo joined her.

When she turned her head to him, he claimed her eager lips once more. Oh, yes, this was most definitely what she needed. He was what she needed…as much as her lungs needed oxygen.

That evening, she let go of all her worries about the DNA tests, the plans for the royal wedding and the future of her business. Lying there wrapped in Leo's very strong, capable arms, all she could think about was him, her, them.

All the problems could wait. Right now, there was a driving need to see where their star-studded night would take them.

CHAPTER FOURTEEN

LAST NIGHT HAD been amazing, spontaneous and unforgettable.

But in the light of day, she knew it had been a mistake.

Bianca groaned in frustration. Her heart said one thing while her mind said the opposite. All her insecurities floated to the surface.

She paced back and forth on the balcony of her room. What had she been thinking to let down her guard and make love to the prince? For a moment, the memory of the night before came rushing to her mind. Leo had been so gentle with her, so loving and thoughtful.

But it hadn't been all sweet and tender. There had been some heady passion that left her utterly breathless and begging for more. It was a night that she would never forget. But it couldn't happen again—no matter how much she wanted to relive it.

It had been a mistake.

She'd put everything she held dear in jeopardy for a man that was out of her reach. She wasn't royal. She didn't have an aristocrat cell in her body. And worst of all, she had the DNA test weighing over her. When it came back and proved she wasn't a Bartolini, who would she be?

She certainly wasn't going to ask Leo to go through this nightmare with her. It wasn't fair to him. This was her burden to carry on her own.

Bianca stopped pacing. She knew what needed to be done. The sooner, the better.

She headed out the door. She knew where to find Leo—in his royal office. On her way, she practiced what she'd say to him.

The clean-cut, always proper assistant stopped typing on his desktop and turned to her when she arrived. "May I help you?"

"I need to speak with the prince."

In total sincerity, Michael asked, "Do you have an appointment?"

In her rush, she hadn't thought of that. She didn't usually have to see Leo during business hours. "No, I don't. But this won't take long."

"I'm sorry. The prince has asked not to be disturbed."

She wondered what that was all about. Did it have something to do with what had happened between them last night? Or did he normally ask for privacy while he worked?

She wanted to ask but it was none of her business. Instead she said, "Thank you."

Just as she was about to turn away, Michael said, "I could give him a message."

She shook her head. This was something that

needed to be said in person. “I’ll speak with him later.”

She moved to the doorway and started down the hallway when she heard her name called out. She paused and turned to find Leo standing there.

He rushed to catch up with her. “Did you need to speak to me?”

“I did.”

“What did you need?” His voice and expression were neutral so she wasn’t able to figure out what he was thinking.

She glanced around as people passed through the spacious hallway. Offices lined both sides of the hallway. There was absolutely no privacy. “Not here.”

“Then come to my office.”

In his office, it’d be easier to stick to the matter at hand. She wouldn’t let herself get distracted with how good his lips felt pressed to hers—

She halted her meandering thoughts. This was what she feared would happen when they were together. She needed to make this meeting short and straight to the point.

“Let’s go.” Her stomach shivered with nerves, but that didn’t stop her from leveling her shoulders and following him.

Once they were in his office with the door closed, she turned to him, finding that he was standing closer than she’d been expecting. She swallowed hard. “It’s about last night—”

"I wanted to speak with you about that too."

"You did?" Her gaze met his.

He nodded. "Yes. But you go first."

This was it. All those practiced words fled her. And now she was left scrambling for a way to phrase this that would leave them in as good a place as possible.

Drawing upon the calm exterior she used for her wedding planner position, she lifted her chin just a bit. "Last night…it was a mistake."

"It was…"

Was that a question? Or was he in agreement? She wasn't able to discern his intent. Her heart raced, pumping her body with nervous energy.

"I shouldn't have let things get out of control," she said.

"You think we are better off sticking to our working relationship?"

"You do understand, don't you?"

He didn't say anything for a moment as though absorbing what she said. "So you would like to pretend like last night never happened?"

"Yes. Exactly."

There was some emotion reflected in his eyes, but before she could define it, he blinked and his feelings were locked behind a wall of indifference.

"We will forget it ever happened."

She held out her hand to him. "Then we have an agreement that our relationship will be nothing but business?"

His thumb stroked the back of her hand, sending tremors of yearning flooding her system. He looked at her with desire in those warm brown eyes.

"Be careful what you ask for," he said. "You might end up regretting it."

She was already regretting many things—none of which were spending those precious hours wrapped in his arms or tasting his addictive kisses. She was in trouble. Big trouble.

The week was getting away from him.

And nothing was going right.

First, the fact that his fling with Bianca was over before it'd really begun bothered him.

Second, his mother was on his case every chance she had, pushing him for the name of his chosen bride. There was little more than a week until his sister said "I do" and his engagement would be announced to the kingdom. His fate would be sealed.

And Leo was not ready. In the beginning, it'd appeared to be an easy enough task. Find a friendly woman whose goals aligned with his. They'd marry, he'd become king and the rest would hopefully fall into place. But somewhere along the way, the gravity of this decision had set in.

Maybe it was seeing how happy his sister was with William. Or maybe it was how happy he was in Bianca's company. Or perhaps it was that magical night beneath the fireworks. Whatever it was, he couldn't settle for mere tolerance of his wife. There had to be more…

His mind filled with the image of Bianca smiling and laughing. How it filled him with such warmth. He recalled their many meals together and though they'd started off discussing his sister's wedding, they'd eventually end up on a far more personal note. Those were the sort of experiences he wanted to share with his wife. Was that asking too much?

But if he didn't make a decision and soon, his mother would take the matter into her own hands. His hands clenched. This was an utterly impossible situation.

And he'd only compounded the matter by acting upon his growing feelings. How was he supposed to choose a wife when all he could think about was Bianca?

Leo frowned as it was now early Friday morning and he hadn't seen or spoken to Bianca since their business lunch yesterday. She'd kept her word about their relationship being all business. He didn't like it. He didn't like it at all. And that's why he'd planned something special for them this morning.

Knowing Bianca was an early riser, he went to find her. It took a bit but he finally tracked her down in the library with his mother. It definitely wasn't the ideal place to meet up with her, but he was determined to see her. His surprise couldn't wait.

The doors were open and he slowed as he heard his mother's voice.

"And why are we supposed to take your advice when you dress like—like that."

Without missing a beat, Bianca spoke up. "Pardon me, ma'am. But this isn't about my personal tastes. We're talking about the princess and what she would like for her wedding. And I must say your daughter has exceptional tastes. She must take after you."

"I, uh, thank you." There was a slight pause as though Bianca's compliment had knocked his mother off her game. But the queen was quick and she soon had the conversation back on track. "However, the princess will wear my wedding dress."

He recognized the stern tone of his mother's voice. She was in no mood to bend or be persuaded from her decision.

Leo stepped into the room. "There you are." His gaze settled upon Bianca just as her mouth was opening to argue with his mother. "We have a meeting."

"We do?"

"Yes."

"But—"

"Leopold, don't forget you are to have lunch with Elizabeth." The queen arched a penciled brow.

"I haven't forgotten. Plans have changed." He was tired of his mother's constant interference. Today, he was going to do what he wanted to do, not what he was expected to do. "Are you ready to go, Bianca?"

Bianca's confused gaze moved between mother and son. Her mouth opened but nothing came out. That was a first.

A smile pulled at Leo's lips. "We don't want to be late." He turned his attention to his mother. "Please excuse us."

His mother looked exasperated. She waved them off.

Once out in the hallway, Bianca stepped in front of him. She glared at him. "Why did you interrupt my meeting with your mother?"

"I was doing you a favor."

"A favor?" Her voice rose with agitation.

He took her hand in his. They moved swiftly down the hallway. It wasn't until they were out of earshot of his mother that he stopped. Bianca yanked her hand free as she shot him another angry glare.

"I'd appreciate if you would let me do my job," she said. "And we don't have any plans."

"That's where you would be wrong."

"No. I'm not." She reached for her phone and ran her finger over the screen. Then she turned the phone to him. "See, I don't have you on my calendar."

"Then your calendar must be wrong."

"My calendar is never wrong. It's what keeps my life, my business, on track."

He wasn't going to argue the point. He had more important matters in mind. "My car is waiting for us. This way."

"And if I refuse?"

"You'll regret it. I promise you're going to love this." He could tell by the widening of her eyes that she was hooked.

Did he have to interrupt her meeting with the queen?

She'd just started to make some headway.

Bianca admitted that she might have pushed the queen hard, but someone had to stand up to her. Otherwise the queen was about to roll right over her daughter. It was Bianca's job to make sure that didn't happen.

When she went to speak to Leo, she realized he was already walking away. She rushed to catch up with him. His long legs took lengthy strides and she had to take two steps for every one of his.

"Do you mind telling me where we're going?"

"Out." He stopped and opened the door for her.

She stepped out into the cool morning air. The sun was shining in the cyan blue sky. There wasn't a cloud in sight. It was going to be a beautiful day.

When Bianca lowered her gaze, she noticed a sleek black sports car sitting in the middle of the drive. It wasn't a new model. This car was a classic but in mint condition. The top was down, revealing its black leather bucket seats. It looked perfect for cruising around and taking in the sights. Not that she had time for sightseeing.

As though Leo had read her thoughts, he moved to the car and opened the passenger side door for her. Just then her phone vibrated in her hand. Her breath hitched as she wondered if it was a message about the DNA results. She glanced at the phone, willing the results to be in—so she'd at last know if she was a true Bartolini…or not.

However, the text message on her phone was from Sylvie. The replacement linens were to be delivered that afternoon. Though it was good news so far as the wedding, she was still left wondering about the DNA results and how they would change her life.

"Bianca? Hey Bianca?"

She glanced up to find Leo waving at her. She pressed her lips into a firm line as she sent off a quick text to her assistant, thanking her for following up on the order.

"Sorry. I have a lot going on right now."

"Exactly why you need a little break."

"You aren't going to let this go, are you?"

"Not until you come with me."

She climbed into the car. The leather seats

were so soft it felt as though they'd been wrapped around her. After Leo climbed in the driver's seat, he fired up the powerful engine. It purred, but Bianca sensed the purr was deceptive. A little pressure on the accelerator and they roared off, down the driveway.

As he adjusted the rearview mirror, she asked. "Are you allowed to do this?" When he glanced at her with a questioning arc of his brow, she added, "You know, go off on your own. After all, you're the crown prince."

A smile lit up his face. Oh, my, was he handsome. Her heart swooned. The traitorous thing.

"It took a lot of negotiating but I've been allowed a certain bit of freedom."

"I bet the queen wasn't happy about that."

He laughed. The sound was warm and rich. "It's not the queen that I had to convince. It was Sir George."

"Who is Sir George?"

"He's the head of my security detail. In fact, he's the head of the royal protection for the palace and the family. But he personally oversees my protection and I've been a challenge to him over the years."

"And he agreed that you could go out driving by yourself?"

"Hardly. Behind us is a dark SUV filled with heavily armed guards. If anyone were to stop this vehicle, they would have an ex-military team to deal with. I can assure you, we are quite safe."

The low-set car clung to the road as they whipped around the mountainous curves. Bianca's hand tightened around the door handle. It'd been a long time since she had been in a sports car. She remembered not long after her brother started to drive that he would be given the task of driving her to visit with friends. He drove so fast, as though he were a race car driver, only he'd had a lot less experience at the time than Leo had now.

Still, Enzo had been a good sport. Without him, she wouldn't have been able to see her friends since they lived so far apart. And her parents were always busy. Her father with the winery and her mother with the horses and the gardening. None of which interested Bianca all that much.

But Enzo made sure she didn't get forgotten in the rush of everyday life. She smiled at the memory. Maybe the distance between them now was something that could be overcome. Maybe they could be close once more. She didn't realize until that moment that it was something she wanted, something she wanted as much as—no, more than—she wanted to win the contest.

"What are you thinking about?" Leo's voice interrupted her thoughts.

"My family. Actually, my brother."

"And that made you smile?"

"Yes, it did. Riding in this sports car reminded me of him when I was a kid and how he would drive me around so I could see my friends. I'd forgotten about it—about how we'd crank up the music and I would sing at the top of my lungs. He'd laugh and we, well, we just had fun."

"And you two don't have fun any longer?"

She glanced down at her hands. "We haven't in a lot of years. We drifted apart when I was a teen. I was more worried about my hair and my clothes than hanging out with my family."

"Isn't that normal for a teenage girl?"

She shrugged. "Maybe. But once the distance was there, we were never able to overcome it."

"By the smile on your face when you thought of your brother, I don't think it'll be hard to repair your relationship."

"It might be harder than you're imagining." And then the story of finding her mother's diary and the fact that one of the three siblings was not a Bartolini by blood all came spilling out.

She didn't know why she'd confessed to Leo. She'd been intending to keep the secret until the DNA results proved what she already surmised—she wasn't a Bartolini. But it felt good to get it out—even if the results were not what she wanted for herself or either of her siblings.

Leo took his gaze off the road for a moment to glance at her. Sympathy reflected in his dark eyes before he focused back on the road. "You shouldn't assume you are not a Bartolini. It could be any one of you. Or maybe you misunderstood—"

"There was no misunderstanding." Bianca wrung her hands. "It makes sense that it's me." Her voice crackled with emotion. "I never lived up to my parents' expectations. I always marched to a different drummer. I wasn't like my brother or sister."

He reached out and took her hand in his. "It doesn't mean you aren't a Bartolini."

"If only that were the truth," she muttered under her breath.

Leo gave her hand one last reassuring squeeze. And then the car pulled to a stop.

She glanced around. "Where are we?"

"This is the best view of the palace and the surrounding area. I like to come up here just to get away from all the pressures. Though I don't get time to do that very often these days."

"I can see why you'd want to come up here. The view is stunning." She stared out at the land as the sun's early morning rays highlighted it. She reached for her phone and snapped a photo through the open window.

When she went to open her car door, he said, "Wait. I have an even better view for you."

"Better than this? Impossible."

"Trust me." He started driving again.

They moved further along the tree-lined road. The car climbed a gradual rise and at the top, a rainbow of color came into sight. It hovered there in all its big, bright brilliance. As the car moved closer, more color was revealed, and soon Bianca realized what she was looking at—a hot air balloon.

"Oh, look." She lightly clapped her hands together in excitement. "I just love hot air balloons. Do you think they'll fly it while we're here?"

Leo pulled the car to a stop. "We can ask."

"Do you know these people?"

He offered only a smile in response. What did that mean? Was he going to use his status as prince to get what he wanted?

As soon as the thought crossed her mind, she felt guilty. In all the time she'd known Leo, he'd never once abused his position as the crown prince. He was better than that.

Leo was a good man. No. He was a great man with a generous, caring heart. When it came time for him to take over the throne, the country of Patazonia would be very lucky.

Her door swung up, startling her from her thoughts. She glanced up to find Leo standing there.

"Are you coming?"

"Of course." She alighted from the car and walked beside Leo.

She thought they would be moving toward the edge of the mountainside for a view of the area, but Leo was headed for the hot air balloon. Suddenly she started to worry that he was doing this for her.

"Leo, we shouldn't interrupt them. They look busy."

"It'll be okay. I'm sure they won't mind letting us take an up-close look."

He took her hand in his. A rush of tingles started in her fingertips and worked their way up her arm. They settled in her chest and had her heart racing.

In that moment, her awareness of their bodies touching—of the smoothness of his palm brushing over hers—was all she could think about. Did he mean something by the touch? Did he need the connection of their laced fingers? Did he crave it like she did?

She felt like a girl once more with the biggest crush on the most popular guy in school. Only Leo was so much more than that—he was an intriguing puzzle of contradictions. And she wanted nothing more than to figure him out.

Leo released her hand to go and speak to the three-man crew filling the balloon. Two men, one on each side, held up the opening of the balloon, while the third man worked the controls. A blast of flames would shoot forth filling the balloon with hot air. It was marvelous to watch as the colorful material rippled and expanded. Up and up it went.

And then Leo was once more by her side, taking her hand in his. "Come on."

She walked with him. “Leo, are we allowed to get this close?”

“We are.”

And the next thing she knew, she was being helped inside the basket. Her heart raced. This was the experience of a lifetime. She was never going to forget this—or the very special man sharing this experience with her.

CHAPTER FIFTEEN

THIS WAS DEFINITELY one of his better ideas.

Leo stood at the edge of the basket as Bianca filmed the lush landscape with her phone. The truth was that he hadn't noticed the passing scenery as he was entranced with the beautiful woman next to him.

Was it wrong that he was supposed to be looking for an appropriate wife and yet all he wanted to do was kiss Bianca? There was something about her—something that drew him to her. She filled his thoughts when he was supposed to be working, when he was supposed to be getting to know some young woman—he was always comparing them, and when he was alone at night, his thoughts were all about her.

He shoved aside his problems. Right now, all that mattered was making Bianca happy.

His gaze moved to her. The big smile on her face was brighter than the morning sun. And there was a gravitational pull to her that drew him close.

"Are you enjoying yourself?" he asked.

She lowered her phone. "I can't believe you did this." Her eyes glittered with happiness. "It's amazing. I love it. Thank you."

Oblivious to the pilot firing the flame to keep them aloft, Leo leaned toward Bianca and pressed his lips to hers. It was a quick kiss, but it had a big effect on the pounding of his heart.

If only they didn't have an audience, he would pull her into his arms and kiss her deeply and thoroughly. Her sweet, sweet kisses were addictive.

She pulled back and gazed up at him with her big round eyes. "What was that for?"

He shrugged, not sure what she was thinking. "Just seemed like the right thing to do in the moment."

A hint of smile pulled at her berry-red lips as she turned her head to the magnificent view. He gazed at the distant horizon, but all he could see in his mind's eye was Bianca.

All too soon the balloon lowered toward a large field not far from the palace grounds. The first touch-down was gentle. It was the second touch-down that jolted the basket and had Bianca reaching out to him to help steady her. He held on to the basket with one hand and placed an arm around her waist with the other arm. She melted into his side, her curves aligning with him as though they'd been made for each other. Her arm wrapped around him too as her other hand white-knuckled the edge of the basket.

When the basket came to a final rest, the relief was written all over Bianca's face. The chase vehicle hadn't caught up to them. Leo helped Bianca from the basket.

In the distance, they heard a vehicle approaching.

"That must be our ride," Leo said.

"You think of everything."

"I try." He sent her a smile, hoping she'd send one back. And she did.

There was no way he wanted this morning to end. And then a thought came to him. As soon as they got back to the palace, they could share a leisurely brunch. He liked that idea. Anything that kept Bianca close by appealed to him.

When he turned back, he noticed the vehicle rushing toward them wasn't a palace vehicle. And there were more vehicles behind it. When someone leaned out the passenger window and started yelling, Leo knew they were in trouble. Without his security team, they were in serious danger.

"Come with me." Leo took her hand in his and headed for the wooded area.

"Leo, what are you doing?"

"That's the paparazzi." At least that's who he hoped it was and not some anti-government group. "We have to go."

For several moments they ran, moving through the thick underbrush. He knew where he was going. He just hoped the paparazzi didn't know these woods.

"Leo?" Bianca called out in a breathy voice. "Leo, please stop."

He came to a complete halt and turned to her. "Are you okay?"

"I... I just need to catch my breath." She huffed and puffed. "I didn't know we were going for a morning run."

"I'm sorry." He felt terrible that their wonderful excursion was ruined. "I never meant for this to happen. Sometimes I forget that I'm a target for headlines."

"Do you think they got a photo of us?"

"I'm not sure. If they did, it was from a distance. Don't worry about it."

"And do you think they're following us?"

He didn't want to think that was true. But he knew that the paparazzi would go to great lengths to get a good photo or a juicy story.

"It's not far from here. Can you keep going?"

She nodded. "But could we slow down a little? The ground is uneven and there are roots sticking up."

He glanced around as he strained to hear any sign that they'd been followed. "I think we're good."

"Maybe you should call someone. Your security will be worried."

He pulled out his phone, but there was no reception out here in the middle of nowhere. "I can't call now, but I will as soon as we get back."

"Then we better get moving before the queen sends out every guard on the palace grounds."

They set off once more at a much more reasonable pace. He told himself he kept ahold of Bianca's hand to help her along the way.

Twenty or so minutes had passed when Leo came to a stop. He released Bianca's hand. She didn't say anything. He could tell she was tired and definitely not happy. The entire day had been ruined. And it was his fault for not doing a better job of planning ahead.

He knew there was an entrance around here somewhere. The problem was that it hadn't been used in so many years there was a significant amount of overgrowth.

He pulled on the vines and at last he found the bars over the entrance. "Here it is."

Bianca moved to his side. "What is it?"

"An entrance to the palace."

Bianca started to laugh. "You can't be serious. It looks like a drainage pipe."

"That's what it's supposed to look like."

"But I'm confused. Why would you want the entrance to the palace to look like a neglected drainage pipe?"

"Because it's a secret entrance."

He hunched down as he worked to release the lever that held the iron grate in place. There had been so many years of disuse and rain that it was rusty. Leo made a mental note to have someone come out here discreetly and make sure it was in better working order.

It took several minutes and all his might, but finally the latch gave way. And then he pulled the grate open.

He stepped inside and then turned back for Bianca. "Come on."

She shook her head. "I… I don't think so."

"Trust me. This a lot shorter than climbing the hillside to the palace."

"But there might be snakes or worse in there." She visibly shuddered.

"What's worse than a snake?"

Softly she uttered, "A spider."

He wanted to tease her, but he saw the genuine fear in her eyes. Instead he pressed a hand to his heart. "I swear upon my life that I will protect you from any snake or spider."

"You think I'm silly."

He shook his head. "Everyone is afraid of something."

"That's not true." Her gaze searched his. "You aren't afraid of anything."

Oh, there was something he feared. But it wasn't some eight-legged creature or the fangs of a reptile, no, what he feared went much deeper.

He feared having his heart broken again. He feared speaking too loudly—too harshly. The image of his father clutching his chest came to mind. If only he'd done what was asked of him—

if he hadn't made waves—then maybe his father would still be here with them. Not wanting to delve further into the subject, Leo didn't correct her.

Using the flashlight app on his phone, he guided them through the tunnel until they came to a steel door with a keypad. He punched in the security code. The heavy door swung open with ease.

He stood aside and waved Bianca into the secure tunnel. He followed her, pausing to press the button for the door to swing shut behind them.

"We are safe now. No one can get in here." He took the lead, using his memory to lead them to the lower level of the palace—the old portion that no one bothered with anymore.

They walked in silence. After a series of turns and a few flights of steps, they'd reached the end. Leo released the catch on the secret movable wall panel. It took some effort, but he finally got it open.

He'd just stepped out into the hallway when he heard: "Leopold. There you are." He didn't have to turn to know it was the queen. And she was none too happy with him.

He inhaled a deep breath and then turned. "Mother."

It wasn't just the queen facing him. There were a half-dozen royal guards behind her. This was bad. Very bad.

The queen turned to the guards and dismissed

them. Once they were gone, she turned back to him. Anger lit up her eyes like little bolts of lightning.

"What is the meaning of this?"

"How did you even know about this passageway?"

She arched a penciled brow. "Leopold, there isn't much around this palace that I don't know about. I've known about the secret passageways since your father took me through them when we were first married. Did you really think I didn't know about your adventures when you were a kid? I'd have thought you would have grown out of such things."

"I didn't have a choice today. The chase team was delayed and instead the paparazzi tracked us down. Do you really think it was a good idea to hang out and let them come up with whatever scandalous drivel sells their papers?"

"I suppose not. But did you stop to think about this before putting yourself in such a precarious position?" She didn't wait for him to answer. "Taking off on a hot air balloon ride of all things when there is work waiting for you. Not to mention—"

Bianca stepped out of the shadows of the secret passageway and stood next to him. The queen's gaze settled on Bianca as her frown grew deeper.

Leo cleared his throat. "I wanted to give Bianca a view of the land. And what better way than from above."

The queen crossed her arms, as though preparing for war.

Leo rushed on. "It was a beautiful morning. But I'm sure Bianca has to get back to work."

Bianca was spurred into motion. "I do. There's a gown fitting shortly. I should go and make sure everything is on track."

When Bianca went to move, the queen spoke up. "Not so fast. I would appreciate it if going forward you would curtail yourself to your work. That is what my son is paying you a fortune for, is it not?"

Leo considered telling his mother that technically he wasn't paying Bianca much, but then he decided that information might work against them. His mother might use it as an excuse to send Bianca packing.

"I assure you, ma'am, that everything for the wedding is on track," Bianca said before Leo could figure out the best way to placate his mother. "I have a checklist to keep us on a timely schedule."

"I hope that list doesn't include any fashions like that." The queen gestured to Bianca's white skinny capris and colorful top.

It wasn't the first time his mother pointed out that Bianca's fashion sense didn't align with hers. The truth was Leo enjoyed Bianca's colorful outfits. This palace certainly could stand to be brightened.

"I like Bianca's sense of style," Leo said, taking

the heat off Bianca. "I'm hoping she'll add color to the wedding."

"Leopold—"

"Mother, not everything should be a shade of gray. Sometimes there needs to be bright oranges, pinks and purples. In fact, purple would suit you."

The queen remained quiet for a moment, not used to Leo getting in her face and disagreeing with her. The quietness didn't last for long. "Then maybe she should pay more attention to her color choices instead of taking up your time. You have other matters of great importance—"

"Bianca," he said, cutting off his mother because he knew where this conversation was headed, "would you mind leaving my mother and me alone so we can talk?"

"No problem." Bianca nodded to the queen and then quietly escaped.

Lucky her. Leo wished he could follow her.

He turned his attention back to his mother. "I know you're frustrated with me but that's no reason to take it out on Bianca. She's doing a really good job with the wedding and Giselle is happy. Isn't that the important part?"

"You're falling for her."

"Bianca?" He shook his head. "No. I'm not."

It was just a passing attraction, nothing serious. When this wedding was over, she'd return to Italy. And he would get on with his royal duties. First, he would get married. And then he would ascend to the throne. It was all planned.

His mother's gaze searched his. "Do you really believe that?"

"Bianca is nice. And I enjoy her company, but that's all it is."

His mother sighed. "Then you are a fool. And I didn't raise a fool."

Without another word, she turned and walked away, leaving him alone with her words. Was she right? Did his feelings for Bianca go deeper than he allowed himself to believe?

CHAPTER SIXTEEN

LAST NIGHT HAD been the most boring date of his life.

And his lunch date wasn't faring much better.

Neither woman would do as his princess.

Leo set aside his now-empty coffee cup. When he glanced up, he found his luncheon companion staring at him. Immediately she smiled at him, like that was going to change things.

There was no spark between them. There wasn't even a fizzle. There was nothing. No chemistry. No anything.

Bridgette was the daughter of an earl of a small country in the Mediterranean. And though many had gone on about her beauty, all Leo could think was that she didn't hold a candle to Bianca's glittering eyes and her sparkling smile.

And then there was the fact that conversation between him and Bianca flowed easily. He didn't have to work to keep the conversation going like he did tonight. How was he supposed to marry someone when they had nothing to talk about?

Bridgette lit up with a smile. "This has been the most enjoyable evening."

She surely couldn't mean it. After all, they

hadn't found one subject to talk about that they had in common.

"It was a nice meal. And I enjoyed your company." Was it wrong that in his mind he pretended he was speaking to Bianca?

"I've heard so much about your lovely gardens."

He followed her over to the glass doors that led out to the expansive patio on the edge of the famed gardens. All the while, he was thinking of how to get out of this. Because he knew as sure as he was standing there that they didn't have a chance for a future. There was no point in getting Bridgette's hopes up.

"Leo, there you are." Giselle rushed into the room. "I've been looking everywhere for you."

"Well, you've found me."

She glanced over at Bridgette. "There's a problem with the wedding."

"What sort of problem?"

Giselle shook her head. "I can't tell you. You have to come see."

"Now?" He knew his sister could get excited about things, but something felt off here.

"Yes, now. Right now—"

"We'd be happy to help," Bridgette interjected as though they were already a couple.

"Um, no. Sorry," Giselle said. "This is delicate and only my brother can handle it."

It was then that Leo glanced toward the interior doorway to find the butler waiting in the wings.

His sister had planned this. And for once, he was grateful for his sister's schemes.

"Then let's go," he said. Before walking off, he turned to Bridgette. "It was lovely meeting you. Thank you so much for making the journey here. Oscar will see you out."

He turned and walked with his sister toward the door. They were just steps away from the hallway—

"Wait. That's it?" Bridgette called out from behind him. "I got all dressed up for this? We didn't even kiss. How are we supposed to get married if you won't even kiss me?"

Giselle grabbed his arm. "Don't you dare stop. If you saddle me with her as my sister-in-law, I will never speak to you again."

Leo smothered a hearty chuckle as they set off down the hallway, but he couldn't resist smiling. "So is there truly an emergency? Or did you simply feel sorry for me?"

Giselle shrugged once more. "There's only so much anguish I can watch my brother endure."

"You were watching us?"

"No. I mean I saw you through the doorway and then I inquired about your guest. When I found out it was Bridgette, I knew you were in trouble."

"You know her?"

Giselle shrugged. "We've met up before at various events. I know all I want to about her and trust me, she's not right for you."

"Maybe I should have you sort through my stack of possible brides."

Giselle stopped walking and frowned at him. "You're making a mistake."

"I'm not any happier about this than you are. But you know I have to marry in order to take the throne. They need to know there's a good possibility of an heir. I am doing what is expected of me. I've put it off as long as I can."

"You need to marry someone you love. Someone you trust. Someone who makes you smile."

He rubbed the back of his neck and glanced away. "That's a luxury I can't afford."

"It's a necessity you would be wise not to overlook."

"Since when did you become an expert on marriage? You haven't even said 'I do' yet." He regretted the words as soon as they slipped past his lips.

Pain reflected in his sister's eyes but in a blink, it was gone. "I have to go."

"Giselle, I'm sorry—"

"Forget it." She turned to walk away.

"What about the wedding?" he asked. "You know, the problem?"

"There isn't one."

And with that his sister marched off in the opposite direction. He knew she was upset with him and he would have to work on making it up to her.

His phone rang. He immediately answered it,

hoping it was the news he'd been awaiting. And it was. By the time he disconnected the call, he had the perfect excuse to go see Bianca.

He set off with quick strides. With each step, his anticipation grew. He had a surprise for her. Something she was going to love.

"Come with me."

Bianca glanced over her shoulder to find Leo standing in the doorway of the palace's grand ballroom. Her fingers tightened around the stylus and her tablet. She was working on the setup for the reception—the best way to use the space available considering the large number of guests. They'd barely started.

"Hi." She couldn't help but smile. Every time he was around, a bubbly feeling sprang up inside her. "I can't leave now. We're working on some last-minute modifications to the layout of the reception."

He walked up to her and glanced at the tentative setup on her tablet. "Looks good. Let's go."

He grabbed her hand and started walking. Bianca dug in her heels, refusing to move. When he noticed her resistance, he stopped and turned back to her.

"What's wrong?" he asked.

"I told you I'm working."

"I know and I'm sorry, but this just can't wait." His eyes pleaded with her to follow him.

"Wait? What are you talking about?"

"Just come with me."

And then a worrisome thought came to mind. Was there some part of this royal wedding that she'd overlooked?

Her heart clenched with dread. There were so many moving parts to this wedding that it was tough staying on top of anything. But in the end, if she could handle this wedding, she could handle any wedding. The trick was getting the princess down the aisle and then onto the dance floor. It was only then that Bianca would be able to take her first easy breath.

"Tell me," she said. "What's wrong?"

"Nothing is wrong." A smile pulled at the corner of his lips. "In fact, something is very right."

"But I need to finish here—"

"Sylvie," Leo called out.

Immediately, Sylvie dropped what she was doing and rushed over to them. She stopped in front of Leo with rounded eyes and a timid smile. She noticeably swallowed before gazing up at him as though he were some sort of god. "Yes, Your Royal Highness?"

Leo took the tablet from Bianca and handed it over to her assistant. "Could you continue to work on setting up the room?"

"I… I…uh…um…yes." Her eyes rounded like saucers. "Definitely. I'd be honored to, Your Highness."

"Thank you." Then he took Bianca by the hand and led her from the room.

"Leo, what are you doing?"

"We have to go. We don't have a lot of time."

"But I need to tell her what I have in mind for the changes."

At last, he stopped and turned to her. "Do you have it written down?"

"Yes—"

"Of course, you do." He turned and keeping his hand clasped around hers, he headed for the door. "I bet you have your entire life planned out in one big list."

She frowned at the back of his head. "Don't make fun of the lists. They keep everything organized and on time."

His pace didn't slow down. In fact, it might have sped up. "But where is the room for spontaneity and fun?"

She didn't respond at first. She'd been so busy proving herself to her parents and her siblings that even though she didn't have the same interests as them that she could still be a success.

When Leo stopped and turned a questioning look at her, she said, "Maybe I'm not the typical young person. So what if I don't live for Friday nights out on the town with my friends, hitting all of the hot spots. And maybe I didn't vacation in Monaco or sail the Mediterranean, but I've worked hard. I've accomplished a lot. If I hadn't, you wouldn't have hired me. Right?" When he didn't immediately respond, she asked again, "Right?"

He sighed. "Right."

"So then don't diss my lists. You might live your life without the need for organization—but being the crown prince, I can't see that lasting—but I need the lists. They make me feel like I have a handle on things. They make it possible for me not to stress out about everything."

Leo looked at her like he was seeing a whole new side of her. "You really enjoy those lists?"

"I know it might be strange for a lot of people, but yes, I like my lists. I need my lists. If I follow my lists, they'll get me where I need to go."

"Hmm... Perhaps you should start a list of fun things."

Now that was something she hadn't considered before. A list of restaurants she'd like to try out. A list of locations she'd like to visit. She already had a list of movies and television shows that she'd like to watch but as yet hadn't gotten around to them.

"So I'm forgiven?" Leo's voice drew her from her thoughts.

"Um...what?"

"You know, for dragging you away from your work?"

"I still don't even know why you drew my away."

"Can I show you?"

"Well, considering Sylvie looked excited to do anything that you asked, I wouldn't want to ruin it for her." And secretly she was curious to know what was so important to him. "Let's go."

Hand in hand, he led her out to a waiting car. The driver opened the door for them. Before Bianca climbed in, she looked back at Leo. "You aren't driving today?"

"I thought this would be easier."

"Easier? Easier for what?"

"You'll soon see." A big smile lifted the corners of his mouth and lit up his eyes.

Whatever he was up to had him very excited. In fact, she'd never seen him this excited. She wouldn't admit it, but his mood was contagious. After keeping her in suspense, he didn't deserve to see her smile. Two could play this game.

As the unmarked sedan moved out through the service entrance of the palace, no paparazzi noticed their exit. It was rather freeing after seeing how the press camped at the front gates and clambered over the official flagged cars as they emerged from the palace grounds.

Bianca wondered what it was like to live under a microscope. She glanced over at the prince. He didn't seem to let it get to him. But growing up in the spotlight must give him a different perspective versus someone like her who had lived a rather anonymous life.

A part of her felt sorry for him. Because not

only were his greatest achievements on display for the whole world to see, but his failures and heartaches were all out there for people to criticize and dissect.

Maybe being a prince wasn't all it was hyped up to be, but as she leaned back against the buttery soft black leather seat and stared out the window at the passing greenery that was quickly giving way to more buildings, more cars, more people, there were definitely some pluses to this life as well.

Bianca questioned him a couple more times about their destination, but he wouldn't crack. And when the car pulled to a final stop and the driver got out to open their doors, she was confused. Leo donned a dark cap and sunglasses. He looked very mysterious.

She stepped out onto the asphalt, raised a hand to her forehead to block the bright sunlight and gazed around at big nondescript buildings.

She turned a questioning gaze to Leo. "You brought me to the warehouse district?"

He laughed. "Not exactly. Come with me and I'll show you the magic that lurks inside."

Magic and this place didn't seem to go together, but she had to admit he had her full attention now. "Leo, what are we doing here?" And then a worrisome thought came to her. "You don't want to move the princess's after-party here, do you?"

The deep rumble of laughter filled the air. "Bianca, do you trust me?"

"No. I mean… I guess—" She halted her rambling. Why did this man get to her and make her a blubbering mess?

When her gaze met his, she found that no harm had been done. He was still smiling.

They headed toward the side of the building. There was a nondescript door with a red light next to it. As they approached, the light went out.

Leo opened the door and stood aside for her to enter. It was darker inside and it took a moment for Bianca's vision to adjust. She let Leo take the lead. He quickly made his way to a group of people and bright lights.

"What is this?" she whispered while glancing up at the spotlights suspended from the ceiling. Then the cameras came into view. "A television station?"

"Close. It's a sound stage. And they are filming your advertisement for your business."

"What?" She slapped a hand over her mouth when her voice was a little too loud and heads turned in their direction.

Leo's smile lit up his eyes. "I told you I would take care of you. And soon this will be on the internet and network television."

"Quiet on the set," a man called out.

No one seemed to notice that beneath the dark baseball cap was the prince. She stood next to him and watched as a bride entered the scene carrying the biggest, most splendid bouquet of pink and white ranunculus and peonies. They were hands down Bianca's favorite flowers.

Leo guided her over to one of the monitors. It was there that they could see the background. In the distance were the green rolling hills of home. In the foreground was her courtyard. But how?

Her gaze moved to Leo. He sent her a knowing smile. That man was good, very good.

They stood quietly while lines were spoken, scenes and retakes were filmed. Bianca wasn't sure how much time passed as she was totally mesmerized by everything that was going on around her.

Leo had taken her marketing preferences and taken them a step further. As the reality of the situation sank in, it was getting harder and harder for her to stifle her excitement. She wanted to speak. She wanted to celebrate the moment.

This wasn't just any commercial. This was a chance to make her dream a reality. This was going to make her a household name in the wedding world. And it was all thanks to Leo.

She didn't know how to thank him, but she would figure out something special. She just had to think about it for a bit.

During a break, someone nudged the director and then pointed over his shoulder at them. Oops! They'd been spotted.

The director rushed toward them. The man made a big flourish of bowing to the prince. Leo stiffened ever so slightly. If she hadn't been standing so close to him, she never would have noticed. So, all of the pomp and circumstance didn't come so naturally to him. Interesting.

"Your Royal Highness, I didn't know you'd be stopping by today. I hope I haven't kept you waiting."

"Not at all." Leo smiled as though to put the man at ease. "We've enjoyed watching the filming."

"Thank you, sir. Is there anything I can do for you?"

"I would like you to meet Miss Bianca Bartolini. She is the woman behind BB Wedding Dreams."

Again, the man bowed. He took her hand and gave a feathery kiss to the back of it. "It's an honor. I hope when we are finished, you'll enjoy the image."

"I've already enjoyed what I've seen. When I see the film merged with the background, it's like I'm home once more."

"Your home, it's gorgeous. People are going to be clamoring to marry at your lovely villa."

"I hope you're right."

They talked for a few more minutes and then they left, leaving the crew alone to finish their work. Bianca couldn't quit smiling.

As soon as they stepped outside, she turned to Leo. "That was amazing. Thank you. It's more than I ever imagined."

His brows rose. "What were you expecting?"

She shrugged. "I don't know. But certainly nothing that elaborate. And you even filmed my villa."

"I thought it should show people exactly what they'd be missing by not getting married there."

Excitement and anticipation bubbled up in her and she acted without thinking by throwing her arms around Leo for a hug. It was when she leaned into him—when she breathed in his clean, masculine scent—that she realized she'd overstepped. His body remained stiff, as though she'd caught him off guard.

She quickly pulled back. "Sorry. I just lost my mind for a moment there."

"I take it you approve?"

She eagerly nodded her head. "I do."

And now the pressure was on her to do something extra special for him. She just had no idea what that might be. But she would think of something.

CHAPTER SEVENTEEN

Buzz. Buzz.

She didn't have time for phone calls.

Still, Bianca couldn't just ignore the call—not until she knew who was on the other end. She removed the phone from her purse. Her heart stilled in her chest when she saw the name of her family's attorney flash on the caller id.

There was no way this was anything but bad news. She'd been dreading this day for the longest time. And now it was here.

Maybe she should just ignore it. She could let it ring over to her voicemail. After all, today was the royal wedding. Giselle and Leo were counting on her to make this day go smoothly for everyone.

She had to bring her very best game today. She couldn't be upset. But she also couldn't be distracted wondering what the attorney wanted.

With great trepidation, she answered the call. "Hello. This is Bianca Bartolini."

As she said her name, she wondered how much longer she would have a right to it. When all was said and done, would everything about her life be a lie—even her name?

"Ms. Bartolini, this is Lando Caruso," the family's attorney said. "I've spoken with your brother and sister. They've informed me you're out of the country."

"That's correct. I'm working on a wedding."

"I see." His voice didn't give any hints as to what he was thinking. "The reason for my call is that the testing facility says they'll have the DNA result in a couple of days."

"Oh." Her heart was heavy and sank all the way down to her silver heels. Not wanting to have any witnesses to her utter meltdown, she said, "Can you give me the results over the phone?"

"No. The agreement with your siblings was that the results would be revealed when you were all in the same room."

"Right." She recalled making that agreement. It seemed like a lifetime ago.

"How soon will you be returning home? As you can understand, your siblings are quite anxious for the results."

She understood very well. "The wedding is today. I'll be able to fly home tomorrow or the next day."

"Very well. I will arrange to be at the villa on Tuesday. Will that give you enough time?"

"Y-yes." Her stomach shivered with nerves.

They ended the call and then Bianca stood there as though in a trance. This could very well be the end of her life as she knew it. With the results at hand, the stark reality of her future was daunting.

Knock. Knock.

Her future and the uncertainty of that future would have to wait for another time. She had a wedding to oversee. And absolutely nothing was going to go wrong today. She owed both Giselle and Leo her undivided attention.

There was another knock.

"Coming!" She glanced in the mirror to make sure she hadn't forgotten anything. She could do this. Because whether or not she was a Bartolini, she was a wedding planner. No one could take that away from her.

The bride was stunning.

The groom, eh, not too bad.

And the entire wedding had gone off without a hitch.

Leo knew who to thank for making his sister's big day so perfect—Bianca. She'd once again worked her magic. She'd smoothed out the rough edges, covered over the imperfections and highlighted the beauty of the day. The only thing that bothered him was that she'd been so busy he hadn't had a moment to so much as thank her.

But there was another part of this day that he dreaded. It meant the deadline for choosing a wife was at hand. It was like a ticking time bomb. And when it went off, life as he knew it would be over. How was he supposed to spend the rest of his days with someone he didn't love?

Because after spending time with Bianca, he'd realized how he longed to share his life with someone he cared about. Waking up in the morning, eager to see that person. Finding out something exciting and anxiously seeking out that person to share the news.

And then there were Giselle and William. They were so in love. They practically glowed when they were in the vicinity of each other. That's what he wanted for his life. Not a cold, heartless business deal—

"Come dance with me."

Leo turned to find the radiant bride next to him. "I'm not much of a dancer."

"We both know that's not true." She grasped his arm. "Come on."

With this being the formal reception, the music was more sedate. It made dancing and talking much easier, which didn't thrill Leo. His sister was good at reading his moods and he didn't want to get into what was on his mind at the moment. This was her wedding. A time for celebration. Not a time to dissect his life.

"You look beautiful," he said.

"Why thank you. You look pretty dashing yourself. Except for that frown on your face."

"What frown?" He didn't know he was frowning. He forced a smile to his lips. "Better?"

"You don't have to put on a show for me."

His muscles stiffened. "I don't know what you're talking about."

"Yes, you do. Mother gave you a deadline to find a wife and the time is up."

He stopped dancing and looked at his sister. "How do you know?"

She smiled and shrugged. "Mother isn't the only one with spies."

He shook his head. "You weren't supposed to know. This is your big day and it isn't your problem."

They started to dance again. "But I want to help."

"No one can help. At this point, I'm considering putting the names in a hat and pulling out one."

Giselle arched a brow. "You're joking, aren't you?"

Part of him was, the other part was seriously considering the option. "How do you choose a spouse that you don't care about?"

"Do you really need me to answer the question?" When he nodded, she said, "You don't."

"But I have to. I need a wife in order to become king. And I need to step into the role by the New Year. The nation is becoming restless." His gaze searched hers. "Who do you think I should marry?"

"I think the answer is right in front of you. All you have to do is open your eyes."

For a few minutes, they didn't speak. He knew

his sister was referring to Bianca. He'd thought of her too. But she didn't fit into the mold of a princess. She was different from all the other prospective brides.

Still, he could see his future with Bianca. He could imagine waking up next to her each morning. He could see having a family with her—a happy family.

But he knew his mother would not approve. Not by a long shot.

"Stop fighting it," Giselle said, drawing him from his thoughts. "You've fallen hard for her. Anyone can see it. Even Mother."

"Bianca is so easy to get along with. Everyone loves her—except Mother."

"Forget Mother for a second." Giselle stopped dancing and stared at him. "Do you love Bianca? Really love her?"

"I do." There was no hesitation. It was a fact that he hadn't been willing to acknowledge until now.

"Then stop standing here. Go get her."

That was easier said than done. He had no idea where she was and the reception was ending. But he would find her. He would tell her how he felt. And then he had to hope she felt the same way.

CHAPTER EIGHTEEN

THIS WAS IT.

The end.

Sadness assailed Bianca. It was the strangest reaction she'd ever had to the end of a wedding. Not just any wedding but a royal wedding that had received international attention. Her phone was ringing off the hook with people eager to have her plan their big days.

She should be thrilled. She should be out on the dance floor of the after-party celebrating, but instead she'd been busy ironing out small wrinkles in the background, from missing appetizers to a shortage of serving staff.

But now with the party in full swing and the prince's favorite band playing, she spotted him smiling and chatting with his sister and a group of guests. That was all the thanks she needed—

"Miss Bartolini, I'd like to have a word." The queen signaled for her to follow.

Once in the hallway, Bianca bowed her head. "Good evening, Your Majesty."

"It was a lovely day. And that in large part was due to you."

Bianca could hardly believe what she was hearing. The queen had just complimented her. After all the rows they'd had and how the queen was certain Bianca was going to make a disaster of everything.

"Thank you." Bianca didn't know what else to say.

"Perhaps my son should consider hiring you for his wedding." Apparently, Bianca failed to keep the surprise from showing on her face as the queen continued. "So, he didn't tell you that he will be announcing his engagement tomorrow. And his wedding will be later this year."

Bianca struggled to speak. "That's exciting news."

Inside she felt anything but excited. She felt sad. She felt as though she were losing the most special person from her life—not that he was ever hers to start with. Just the thought of Leo with another woman filled her with jealousy. She quickly reined in her rising emotions.

"Very exciting. Everything is working out." The queen beamed with happiness. "I've had my assistant forward you a bonus for your success tonight. And I know you must be anxious to get home to your villa so I've had my jet put on standby. It's yours tonight or tomorrow."

"Thank you. I really appreciate it."

"I won't keep you. Since this party isn't really my style, I'm going to call it a night and let the young people live it up. Goodbye, Miss Bartolini."

"Good night, ma'am." Bianca bowed her head once more.

She watched as the queen made her way to the door. There was nothing left for Bianca to do. Sylvie was seeing to any lingering details.

The thought of flying home tonight was tempting. It would be nice to get back to the villa while she was still a Bartolini—

"Bianca! There you are." Leo stepped out of the party, closing the door behind him. "I've been looking everywhere for you."

"Sorry. There were a lot of things to do today." Like saying goodbye to him. But she wasn't ready to do it. Not yet.

"You did a positively fabulous job. Not even my mother could find anything to complain about."

"I know. She gave me both a compliment and a bonus. Can you believe it?"

Leo's brown eyes widened. "You really impressed her. I am not surprised. Everyone is calling it the perfect wedding. And it's all thanks to you."

She couldn't put on this "nice" show any longer. She had to know if it was true. Was Leo getting married? "And I heard about your engagement." Her voice wobbled. "Congratulations."

Confusion clouded his eyes. "How did you hear—wait, my mother, right?"

She nodded. "She's very excited."

"I didn't want you to find out this way."

"What way? The fact that I thought what we shared meant something and all of this time you were planning to marry someone else—"

"Bianca, stop." He reached out, gently grasping her upper arms. "It isn't like that."

She yanked free. Her gaze narrowed in on him. "How is it?"

"It's you."

"What's me?"

He rubbed the back of his neck. "This isn't how I meant for any of this to happen."

"You aren't making any sense. What about me?"

His gaze met hers. "It's you I want to marry."

She pressed a hand to her chest, feeling as though the air had been sucked from her lungs. "Marry me?"

Leo nodded.

She shook her head. This couldn't be happening. Leo wanted to marry her but she was a wedding planner, not a fitting wife for the crown prince. She was a nobody, a commoner. The prince must marry someone of noble birth.

"No." She took a step back. "You don't mean this. It would be a mistake."

"Bianca, I love you."

She took another step away from him. Her heart was cracking and her vision blurred with unshed tears. "No, you don't."

He stepped up to her. His unwavering gaze met

hers. "I don't know where all of this doubt is coming from, but if you're worried about my mother, don't be. I'll deal with her."

"It's not your mother."

"Good. Then what is it?"

"Will you still feel the same way about me if the DNA results reveal that I'm not a Bartolini? What happens if I don't know who my father is? For all I know, I could be the daughter of a criminal." Her voice wobbled. She blinked repeatedly, struggling to keep her emotions at bay. "I can't marry you with that hanging over our heads."

Silence filled the air between them.

The silence was more painful than acknowledging that everything she thought she knew about herself might be wrong. Because Leo's continued silence meant he agreed with her.

Unable to take the silence any longer, Bianca said, "My job is complete. Sylvie is inside and will oversee the cleanup. I need to go."

The door to the party opened. The blast of music echoed through the hallway. Giselle beamed at them and then yelled over the music. "Come on guys. Let's party." She moved over and latched her arm with Leo's. "I requested your favorite song."

Giselle motioned for Bianca to join them before disappearing inside. Bianca moved toward the door but remained in the hallway. She couldn't go back inside. She closed the door.

This was difficult enough. She just needed to

get it over with. She needed to take the queen up on her offer and return to Tuscany as soon as possible.

Because if she loved Leo—and she did love him with all her heart—she would be on that plane tonight. Leo needed to live the life he was destined for—the throne that he always wanted. He deserved to have a wife by his side that the people looked up to and respected.

And it wasn't her. She probably wasn't even a Bartolini. If she were to marry Leo and the press got ahold of the story it would ruin Leo. She would do anything to protect him, including sacrificing her heart.

The acknowledgment hurt Bianca more than she knew possible. She didn't fit in with her family. She didn't fit in Patazonia. Where did she belong?

CHAPTER NINETEEN

HE'D MESSED UP.

Big time.

Leo had taken time to think about what Bianca had said to him instead of following his heart. In his defense, he never expected her to turn down his marriage proposal. But that was becoming a thing with Bianca—not reacting the way he expected.

By the time he'd gotten his head screwed on straight, Bianca had left the party. He'd quietly slipped away, eager to find her. He had to convince her that they belonged together. Maybe theirs wouldn't be a fairy-tale marriage, but truth be told, he didn't believe in fairy tales.

He wanted a relationship that was real—a relationship that was strong, reliable and enduring. He could have all of that with Bianca. He firmly believed it. In fact, he couldn't imagine his life without her in it.

He demanded the keys to the SUV that his security detail had used to escort him to the reception. He was in no mood to be coddled by his team. He needed some space to himself. He tramped the accelerator. When he found the inside of the vehicle too constricting, he put down the windows and let the cool night air rush over his face as he raced back to the palace.

This can be fixed. It isn't too late.

He kept repeating the mantra the whole way home. It was as if he said it enough, it would be so.

The SUV's tires screeched to a halt in front of the palace. He raced inside. He could feel curious stares from the staff, wondering what had him in such a rush, but he didn't have the patience or the inclination to explain.

He took the stairs two at a time. He racewalked down the hallway. He rapped his knuckles on Bianca's door.

"Bianca?" He waited. No response. "Bianca, we need to talk."

The door opened but it wasn't Bianca on the other side. It was one of the staff.

"Where is Bianca?" he asked, not caring how anxious he might appear. He didn't have time to worry about appearances.

The young woman looked confused. "Miss Bartolini isn't here."

"Do you know where she is?"

"She left."

"Left?" That couldn't be. "As in left the palace? To go back to the party?"

The young woman looked flustered. "I don't know where she went. I was instructed to help her pack and then I started to straighten up. Was that a mistake?"

The mistake was all his. The weight of his error mounted with every passing moment.

Noticing the maid's worried look, he said, "You've done nothing wrong. Continue what you were doing."

He turned and strode away. She'd left already? The after-party hadn't even wound down.

He wasn't giving up yet. He could catch her at the airport. He'd do whatever it took.

Leo retraced his steps down the staircase, but at the bottom stood the queen. "Leopold, what is the meaning of this? You're racing up the driveway, screeching tires and running through the palace as though it's some sort of gymnasium."

He descended the stairs. "It's Bianca. I have to find her."

The queen's brows rose. "Is there a problem with the party?"

"No. It's fine." He raked his fingers through his hair. "There's something I have to discuss with her."

"Well, if that's all, you'll have to phone her because she's already in the air. I gave her my personal jet to return home."

"You did what?" He couldn't believe what he was hearing.

The queen frowned at him. "Come with me."

He followed her to her office, where most of

the kingdom's decisions were made. It was where his ancestors including his grandfather, father and eventually he would rule from. This seemed like a fitting place to have this life-altering conversation.

"I've chosen a wife," he stated boldly. "If she'll have me."

His mother's frown lifted into a smile. "Very good. And I take it you'd like Bianca to plan the wedding. I will admit that she did a pretty good job with your sister's wedding, but you have to realize with you being in line for the crown, traditions must be strictly adhered to—"

"Mother, stop!"

She blinked as though surprised by his interruption. "Leopold, I'm not going to be as agreeable this time. Bianca cannot be your wedding planner."

"You're right. She's going to be my bride."

His mother's penciled brows rose high on her forehead. "Leopold, if you're trying to be funny—"

"I'm being perfectly serious. I want to marry Bianca. I want her to be my princess—"

"Stop! No." The queen vehemently shook her head. "It's not going to happen. I gave you a whole selection of very fine women to choose from. Just because you couldn't find your version of the ideal woman—"

"But I did. Bianca is everything I've ever wanted and more."

His mother shook her head again. "Leopold, you're missing the fact that she doesn't have noble blood. She isn't from a politically influential family. She brings nothing to the nation. She's…she's a wedding planner."

"She's the woman I love. And she loves me in spite of my faults—"

"Faults?" The queen's eyes narrowed. "This woman has convinced you that you are full of faults?"

"No, Mother," his voice filled with pent-up emotion. "You did that the day Father died." His mother's mouth opened but he didn't give her a chance to speak as he kept going. "When he died, you looked at me like it was all my fault. And you've been blaming me ever since."

"That's not true."

"It is true. Whether you admit it or not."

The composed look on her face crumbled. In its place were deep worry lines that aged his mother. She sat down on the window seat as though her legs would no longer hold her up. "I had no idea that's how you felt."

"How could I not when you sent me out of the room after father died as though you couldn't bear to look at me. And you made me promise not to tell anyone what had happened. Do you know what keeping that secret cost me? I couldn't even talk to Giselle."

For so long, he'd kept this torment of emotions

locked up inside of him. But after confiding in Bianca, he realized the secret was destroying not only him but also his relationship with his family. He'd been distancing himself—avoiding conflicts. And it was no way to live life. It was no way to rule a country.

"But you told Bianca?" His mother's troubled gaze searched his.

"I did. I trust her. And I don't regret it."

"And she convinced you that I blamed you for your father's death?"

"On the contrary, she defended you." His mother's eyes widened. Maybe at last his mother would see that there was so much more to Bianca. "She suggested you might have been trying to protect me."

"I was." The queen's voice was soft as though all of the fight had gone out of her. "Our enemies will use anything to hurt us, even twisting innocent facts into something sinister."

He could barely allow himself to believe what he was hearing. "You never blamed me?"

She shook her head. "Your father had health issues."

"I never knew."

"Only four people knew of them. Two of them were your father and myself. A king must not look vulnerable."

Leo had a feeling his mother's last comment was aimed at his relationship with a commoner.

"Bianca will not make me vulnerable. With her by my side, we can do great things together. I love her."

"But does she feel the same way?" The queen stood. "Maybe she doesn't love you and that's why she left so quickly."

"She left because I made a mistake. Now I need to make things up to her."

"You really love her, don't you?" When he nodded, his mother said, "There's a commercial flight tomorrow."

It was his turn to arch a brow. "You aren't going to try and stop me?"

"Maybe I should. But when it all comes down to it, I want my children to be happy. And Bianca makes you happier than I've ever seen you. So go get her. Make her your princess."

"Thank you." He hugged his mother, something they rarely did, but he had a feeling that was about to change. When he pulled back, he said, "You try to put on a crusty exterior but on the inside you're just a marshmallow."

She sent him a playful frown. "Go. Before I change my mind." His mother turned and walked away. She called over her shoulder, "And have someone move that vehicle."

Now he had to wait through the night to get to his princess.

It was going to be the longest night of his life.

CHAPTER TWENTY

"YOU'RE BACK."

It was almost lunchtime when Bianca dragged herself to the main house. She glanced over at Gia as she entered the kitchen. Bianca smoothed a hand over her mussed-up ponytail. She'd forgotten that her sister had turned the place into a boutique hotel and that there might be guests lurking about. She peered past her sister, relieved to find her alone.

"I got in late last night."

Gia had already turned in by then, but Enzo had still been awake. He knew Bianca was upset but he hadn't pried. He just let her know he was there if she wanted to talk.

She turned her back to her sister to avoid questions about the shadows under her bloodshot eyes.

"I loved the photos you sent," Gia said. "Do you have some of the wedding?"

"Um… I do. But not on me." The last thing she wanted to discuss was the royal wedding. "I was so tired last night that I forgot to plug my phone in and now it's dead, kind of like me. Do you have some coffee you can spare?"

Gia made them both a cup and then joined Bianca at the kitchen island. "You don't look so good, considering you just planned the wedding of a lifetime."

And had my heart torn out and shredded.

"How am I supposed to look?"

Gia shrugged. "Like you're on top of the world. The phone has been ringing like crazy with people trying to reach you to plan their wedding."

"Sorry about that."

"Sorry?" Gia studied her. "Now I know something is wrong. Bianca, what is it? Tell me what has you looking like you just lost your best friend."

Bianca needed someone to talk to and so she started at the beginning. She left out some of the steamy bits, some things weren't for sharing. And then the proposal—

"And you turned him down?" Gia's voice rose.

"Shh..." Bianca glanced at the doorway to assure herself that they were still alone. "I don't want anyone to know."

"I wouldn't want anyone to know you lost your mind either. I mean, it's obvious by the look on your face when you mention Leo that you love him. And he's a prince. What else do you need?"

"You don't understand. What happens when the DNA test says I'm not a Bartolini?"

"You're still you and he loves you."

Bianca shook her head. "He loves the idea of me. But when I pointed out about the DNA tests and that I could be anyone's daughter, including a criminal's, he went silent." It was only when her sister's face paled that Bianca realized she'd said too much. "Gia, I didn't mean that. I… I was just being thoughtless."

"It's okay." The look on her face said it was anything but okay. "It's the truth. We don't know anything about the biological father."

Not sure what to say, Bianca opted to distract her sister with her story about Leo. "Anyway, Leo didn't say a word and then he walked away. That was all the answer I needed."

Gia grabbed a tray of pastries and placed them in front of Bianca. "I think you're going to need these." When Bianca arched a questioning brow, Gia added, "You know, comfort food."

Bianca's gaze moved to the tray. "I'm going to need a lot more sweets than this. Do you have any chocolate?"

Before Gia could answer, sounds of a commotion came from the front of the villa. What was that all about? Some rowdy guests?

"I'll be right back." Gia rushed out of the room.

Bianca browsed the cabinets for some chocolate. The voices in the front room grew louder and she could hear Gia's raised voice. Alarmed, Bianca pushed the cabinet door shut and rushed after her sister.

Bianca came to a halt when she spotted Leo. Her heart leaped into her throat.

What was he doing here? Not that she should care. Whatever they'd shared was over.

"Go away."

Leo braced himself for a prickly reception. He just hadn't expected the hostility to come from Bianca's sister. It didn't surprise him. He'd handled things poorly with Bianca. He just needed a chance to make it up to her.

Luckily for him, the private jet had returned earlier than expected and he didn't have time to wait until noon for the commercial flight. It was refueled and ready to go early that morning. Still, it had taken him longer to get to the Bartolini estate than he'd planned because he had to make an important detour. It was a crucial part of his plan to win Bianca back. He hoped it would prove to her once and for all how much he cared about her...if only he could get past her brother and sister.

"I'm not leaving until I speak to Bianca," Leo said as Enzo continued to stand in front of him with his fists pressed into his sides.

"She doesn't want to see you," Enzo said while Gia agreed with him. "I don't care if you are a prince, you can't hurt my sister."

"You don't understand—"

"I understand that my sister was crying and that's all I need to know."

The fact he'd caused Bianca such pain weighed

heavy on him. He had to make it up to her, if she'd let him. "I can fix this."

Gia stepped between the two men. She leveled her shoulders and tilted her chin upward. "If you've come to tell my sister that she's not good enough to be a royal, you can leave now."

That's what she thought? It couldn't be further from the truth. But he didn't want to explain himself to Bianca's siblings. The person he needed to explain things to was Bianca—

"Leo, you shouldn't be here." Bianca stepped into the room.

"Don't worry about him," Enzo said. "He was just leaving."

"No. I wasn't." Leo frowned at the man. And then he turned his attention to Bianca. "I need to speak with you. Alone."

"We have nothing left to discuss."

"Listen, I messed up and I'm sorry." He pulled a huge bouquet of red roses from behind his back. "These are for you."

Bianca's eyes paused on the flowers before meeting his gaze once more. He couldn't read her thoughts. It was as though she'd put up a protective wall and now he had to find a way to breach it.

"Please go, Leo. It's over. It was a mistake." She turned and walked away.

He desperately wanted to follow her—to tell her that nothing was over between them. They were just getting started, but her two protective siblings weren't about to let him get past them.

He placed the flowers on a stand by the door. "I'll be back."

He wasn't giving up. He loved Bianca. And she loved him too. She was afraid of the results of the DNA test and he had to prove to her that they didn't matter to him.

CHAPTER TWENTY-ONE

THE FLOWERS STARTED showing up the next day.

"I don't know where to put them all," Gia said. "It's starting to look like a florist shop in here." Gia looked at Bianca with sympathy in her eyes. "I know he screwed up, big time, but would it hurt to hear him out?"

Before Bianca could answer there was a knock at the door. She didn't have to wonder. She knew who was there—the florist. Again.

Bianca moved toward the door. "Don't worry. I'll have them take the flowers away."

She swung open the door, but the words lodged in her throat. There stood Leo.

"You can't be here," she said. "A guest might see you and it'll end up on social media."

"That's a risk I'm willing to take."

"Why are you making this so difficult?" Every time she saw him, the feeling of loss washed over her. How was she ever going to forget him—her very own Prince Charming?

"Just hear me out. That's all I'm asking. And then if you still want me to go, I will." He could see the indecision reflected in Bianca's eyes. "Please."

"Okay. We can go outside—"

"I have a car." When her eyes widened in surprise, he added, "It's getting late. I thought we could talk over dinner."

"I don't know."

"Go with him," Gia said. "Give him a chance. We don't have room for more flowers."

Maybe it was the best way to set things straight with him. Bianca glanced down at her skinny jeans and purple top. "I should change."

"You look perfect," Leo said. "You're always beautiful."

Meanwhile, her sister stood to the side, urging them out the door.

Bianca said, "A quick dinner and then you'll leave?" When he nodded, she added, "And no more flowers?"

"I promise."

She grabbed her purse and shoes. Then they were out the door. She noticed him messaging someone as they headed toward the car. Then he slipped the phone in his pocket and opened the car door for her.

Why was he making this so difficult?

Bianca's heart ached.

There was nothing that could change things between them. Leo was royalty. She was not. And the DNA tests were delayed so it'd be another few days until they received the results.

Still, her body longed to fall into his strong arms—to rest her cheek against his muscular chest—to hear the steady pounding of his heart. It might have been a little more than twenty-four hours since she saw him last but she'd missed him dearly. How was she going to exist without seeing him again, except for on the front of a glossy magazine?

"We should talk now," she said as the car headed toward Florence.

"Not yet."

"Leo, nothing you say is going to change our circumstances."

"Just wait. We're almost there. And I'd like to be able to look at you when we talk instead of concentrating on the road."

The red sports car he'd rented slowed as they made their way into the city.

"There it is." Leo pulled into a parking spot.

Before she could get out, he'd rushed around the car and opened the door for her. As they started up the sidewalk, she noticed a group of photographers. They started snapping pictures as flashes repeatedly lit up the sky.

Bianca stopped walking. "Leo, we can't go in there."

"Sure we can."

"But the paparazzi—"

"It'll be okay."

"But how did they know you would be here?" She stared at him. Something was up, but what? "I didn't even know you'd be here."

"I told them," he said matter-of-factly.

"You did?" Her words got lost in the frenzy of questions volleyed at them from the reporters.

Leo took her hand and led her through the crowd. At last they were inside the restaurant. They were immediately seated—next to the window.

"Excuse me," Bianca said to the maître d'. "Can we have another table? Away from the window?"

"It's okay," Leo said. "I requested this table."

"You did?" She didn't understand. What was going on?

Leo took her hands in his as they stood next to the table. On the other side of the window flashes went off. But in that moment, as Leo stared into her eyes, he was all she could see. His voice was all she could hear.

"Bianca, I'm sorry about what happened back at the after-party. I didn't react the way I should have. When you started throwing out all those excuses of why we shouldn't be together, I got nervous. But now I want the entire world to know how I feel about you."

"Th-those weren't excuses. They are the truth. I'm not a part of your world. I don't even know what world I belong in. The DNA results—"

"I know where you belong. With me."

Tears stung the backs of her eyes. He was saying all the right things. "But what happens when the DNA results say I'm not a Bartolini? Those reporters out there will have a field day. It could threaten your position as king."

"It doesn't matter. Don't you know how much I love you?"

Her heart pounded in her chest. "But what about when you become king—?"

"I would step down from the throne if that's what it took for us to be together."

"You would?"

He nodded. "I would."

"But the queen—she'll never approve."

"I told her I love you and it took some convincing but she's coming around. I'm sure you can win her over."

How was it that he was overcoming all her objections? Her gaze searched his. "What are you trying to tell me?"

"Bianca, I love you and it doesn't matter about your heritage. I know you have the biggest, most caring heart." He removed a small black velvet box from his pocket and opened it. The camera flashes were now almost continuous. He held the biggest teardrop diamond ring out to her.

A tear of joy splashed onto her cheek. "Leo, what have you done?"

He dropped down on one knee. "Bianca Bartolini, I fell for you the day I saw you at the wedding at the villa. Since then I've come to love your company, your sense of humor and your warm smiles that light up my darkest days. No test is going to change my feelings for you. I love you with all my heart. And I just have one question for you: will you be my queen?"

Her heart pounded with love for this man. It was then that she realized exactly where she belonged—next to the man she loved.

"Yes. Yes, I will. I love you."

He pulled the ring from the box and slipped it on her trembling hand. And then he stood. He peered deeply into her eyes. "You're the most amazing woman. And the people of Patazonia are going to love you as much as I do."

And then he lowered his head and pressed his lips to hers as flashes lit up the entire room. Fairy tales really do come true.

* * * * *

Look out for the next story in
The Bartolini Legacy trilogy
Coming soon!

And if you enjoyed this story,
check out these other great reads from
Jennifer Faye

Her Christmas Pregnancy Surprise
Wearing the Greek Millionaire's Ring
Claiming the Drakos Heir
Carrying the Greek Tycoon's Baby
All available now!